Discover for yourself why readers can't get enough of the multiple award-winning publisher Ellora's Cave. Whether you prefer e-books or paperbacks, be sure to visit EC on the web at www.ellorascave.com for an erotic reading experience that will leave you breathless.

WWW.ELLORASCAVE.COM

BLOOD OF THE ROSE
An Ellora's Cave Publication, May 2004

Ellora's Cave Publishing, Inc.
PO Box 787
Hudson, OH 44236-0787

ISBN #1843609290

ISBN MS Reader (LIT) ISBN # 1-84360-708-5
Other available formats (no ISBNs are assigned):
Adobe (PDF), Rocketbook (RB), Mobipocket (PRC) & HTML

BLOOD OF THE ROSE © 2003 ANYA BAST

ALL RIGHTS RESERVED. This book may not be reproduced in whole or in part without permission.

This book is a work of fiction and any resemblance to persons, living or dead, or places, events or locales is purely coincidental. They are productions of the authors' imagination and used fictitiously.

Edited by SHERI ROSS CARUCCI
Cover art by ROSE HURST.

BLOOD OF THE ROSE

Anya Bast

To Brenda. True friends are rare and precious. Thank you for being mine.

And to Kara. Fly on, my sweet angel.

Prologue
1876 England

Penelope pressed her hand flat against the glass, absorbing the rage of the storm outside. Lightning split the rain-swollen clouds and thunder boomed. She closed her eyes, feeling a kinship with the tumult beyond.

She was a wicked girl. Hadn't her new nanny, Horatia, told her that frequently? Wicked because she liked storms when proper little girls would cower in fear. Because she climbed trees and hunted for frogs when a well-bred young lady sat primly at her lessons. Wicked because her best friend was an Irish stable boy. And, most of all, wicked because she'd been born with a red caul.

The servants had whispered of her red caul since Penelope had been old enough to remember. They said she'd taken her mother's life to come into the world and a curtain of blood had coated her newborn face. Penelope squeezed her eyes shut and rested her forehead against the cool glass of the window. *Of course she was wicked.*

Penelope wished she could leave this place. She didn't belong here with the beautiful, well-behaved people, the perfectly manicured lawns and tended gardens. This environment did not match how she felt inside. Thunder cracked again and she smiled. The storm matched her quite well.

"Penelope!"

She whirled to face Horatia. Her nanny stood with her hands on her slim hips, her salted black hair pulled tight into a bun. Penelope thought the strands must have been choking for want of air.

"Where have you been?" Horatia demanded. She walked toward her with iron-spined grace. Her lips compressed into a thinner line, and her eyes darkened with every step she took. Horatia bent and pinched the collar of Penelope's dress between two fingers. "Absolutely scandalous. You're smeared with mud! You've been running around with that stable boy again, haven't you?"

"Miss Horatia, I—"

"Don't lie to me, girl!"

Horatia yanked her forward, out of the drawing room. "Draw a bath," Horatia snapped at Mrs. Watkins, the housekeeper, who'd been passing through the foyer. Mrs. Watkins glanced at Penelope, her face taking on a look of sympathy. Then she whirled and raced up the stairs to do as Horatia had bid.

Her nanny jerked on Penelope's upper arm and pulled her up the stairs. "I understand your father is too preoccupied to care, and you've no close female relations to be shocked at your behavior, so you must think of me as every female relation you do not have.

I will teach you the way of things, Penelope, and bring you to understand your role and what society expects of a young lady such as yourself."

"Yes, Miss Horatia," Penelope answered.

They entered the gleaming bathroom, decorated with white porcelain and polished dark wood furnishings. Mrs. Watkins had started the water in the bathtub and laid towels and soap upon a chair beside it. The plump housekeeper cast one more sidelong look at Penelope and then bustled out the room.

Water filled the tub as Horatia, muttering to herself angrily all the while, stripped Penelope's clothes and laid them over a chair. Her nanny deposited her in the enameled cast-iron tub now partially filled with warm water. Then Horatia scrubbed a chunk of soap in a wet washcloth and rubbed it hard over her shoulder. Penelope yelped.

"Now that I have been here a week, Penelope, it is time you and I had a serious talk. First of all and without argument, I must insist that you never, ever associate again with that boy your father told me about. Your father has been far too lenient. If you are lonely and you need friends, we will find you suitable ones, children of your father's peers. You will not find your friends in eleven year old Irish stable boys who shirk their duties to corrupt a child!" She let out a quick breath of air and shook her head. "You'll give the lad ideas above his station."

Tears pricked Penelope's eyes. Give up Aidan? But she felt right with him. He listened to her when she spoke and cleaned her up when she skinned her knee. He protected her.

"I will see the boy later today and explain this to him in no uncertain terms. He is simply *not good enough* to keep your company, Penelope." Horatia sighed in exasperation. "It is beyond scandalous. It's a good thing your father hired me. At eight, you're far too old for such behavior. A few years older and you'd be ruined. The servants already gossip."

"But—"

"You are Miss Penelope Agnes Coddington," Horatia reminded her. "The daughter of Jeffery Coddington and sole heir to his wealth and estates. Such a girl does not wallow in the mud with common servant children. You want to make your father proud you are his daughter, don't you? You will not accomplish that by associating familiarly with those beneath you."

Penelope sniffled and yelped again as Horatia pulled her hair in an effort to lather it with the soap.

"If you cannot accept the responsibilities of being Mr. Coddington's daughter, perhaps you should leave the luxury of your father's house and go to live in the servant quarters. They can teach you *other* responsibilities. Responsibilities perhaps better suited to you, for example, mucking out the stalls and doing the wash. Would you like that?"

Penelope didn't answer. Her fingers curled around the edge of the bathtub as she held on under the onslaught of the rough washcloth Horatia wielded. Soap dripped into her eyes, stinging them.

Horatia plugged Penelope's nose, then dunked her under the water to rinse the soap from her hair. Even under the water Horatia's garbled diatribe reached her ears. She came up sputtering, her tears mixing with the bathwater. Horatia took the soap in hand once more and started the process again.

"They can teach you more still," Horatia continued. "How to—"

"But Aidan is my only friend," Penelope sobbed. Tears rolled down her cheeks and her lower lip quivered.

Horatia took her by the shoulders, forcing their gazes to meet. "*I* am your friend, Penelope. I will teach you all you need to know to assume your place in this world, to become a proper daughter of England and take your place among society. You do want that, don't you? You do want to make your father proud, to make him love you, don't you?"

Penelope sniffled once and nodded. She wanted her father to love her more than she wanted anything. "Yes, Horatia."

Chapter One
1890

Twigs and dry leaves snapped and crackled under Penelope's polished black riding boots as she marched toward the stables.

"Aidan," Penelope snapped when she strode through the double doors. "Saddle Daisy. I fancy a ride before dinner."

Aidan O'Shea looked down at her a fraction longer than a servant should before moving to take the chestnut mare from her stall. "Yes, miss," he drawled out, casting her a dark sidelong glance. "You know I live to do your bidding."

Penelope's lips tightened into a thin line. It was always so with him. He could never remember his place. It was as if he thought that just because they had been childhood chums, he could take liberties in the way he talked to her. "Thank you," she bit off.

She took her black riding crop from its peg on the wall and dangled it from one finger while she watched Aidan lead Daisy from her stall. His features had always been well formed—his jaw strong, his lips full and nice...when they weren't quirked with sarcasm. He looked less like a servant every day. Indeed, ever since Penelope had grown old enough to notice those of the opposite sex, she'd noticed Aidan. She knew well how scandalous that was, but she couldn't help herself.

He tossed a saddle blanket over Daisy, and Penelope watched as his back muscles worked under his shirt. A hank of glossy brown hair fell over a dark blue eye as he turned toward her, his attention focused on his work. Small curling tendrils of his thick hair brushed the collar of his tan shirt as he moved.

His pants molded to nicely muscled thighs. As a lady, she shouldn't notice the impressive bulge between his legs, but as a woman she couldn't help but let her eyes linger and her mind wonder what he'd look like without his pants. She lifted a brow.

Yes, overall, Aidan was an exceptionally good-looking man. He did not put one in mind of a servant when one gazed at him.

And it was not only his physical appearance that made him appear more like a member of the upper class than a servant; it was his composure and confidence. While the shoulders of the other servants always sagged, his were broad and squared. While a proper servant lowered his gaze when speaking to a member of the Coddington family, Aidan's intense eyes never failed to find hers.

Even now, his midnight blue gaze met hers over the saddle he was cinching around Daisy's midsection. A dark brow rose. "Your father know you're going for a ride?"

"I am not a child anymore, Aidan. I can go riding if I choose." She glanced away. "Anyway, you know he doesn't care if I ride or not."

Aidan nodded while slipping the horse's bit between its teeth and adjusted the thin leather straps over the animal's head. He handed the reins to her. "Your horse, Miss Penny," he said, while looking straight into her eyes just as a good servant ought not.

"Call me Penelope!" she scolded.

At one time, Aidan had called her Penny and she'd liked it, but those times were long past. When she'd been a child and had been lonely, she'd adored Aidan and trotted at his heels. Indeed, when she'd been young she'd been inexplicably drawn to him. She was *still* drawn to him, though she fought it.

Thank goodness for Horatia. She'd taught her to be respectable. Indeed, over the years Horatia's sharp tongue had cut and shaped Penelope into a proper English lady. The bond Penelope and Aidan had seemed to share was quashed before it grew out of control and she sullied her reputation with such foolishness. But their early familiarity had affected Aidan in bad way. Now it was as if he fancied himself an equal. He was never suitably courteous to his betters. Even when he spoke in a pleasing manner, satire always simmered beneath his words.

It just wouldn't do.

She regained her composure and lifted her chin a degree. "You know, you would be better served to address your superiors with care, Aidan. My father was quite charitable in keeping you on after your parents passed away. It is not often we employ the Irish."

His eyes got that dangerous dark glint in them. The look that made her stomach do flip-flops. She pulled her gloves from her pocket and pulled them on to distract herself.

"And isn't that ironic seeing as how you got a wee bit o' the Irish in you," Aidan responded, exaggerating his accent simply to irk her, she knew.

Penelope's attention snapped from her gloves up to Aidan's face. One fat sausage curl that had caught on the button of her jacket pulled free and bounced against her chin. "I most certainly do not!"

He smiled lazily, showing the dimple in his cheek. "Then what of the bit of red in your hair then, or the green of your eye? How do you explain those away, miss? Other than the possibility that one of your ancestors dallied a bit with one of their servants and you inherited their characteristics?"

Penelope's mouth opened in a silent 'O' of surprise. Aidan had hit a sore spot with her. Both of her parents were exceedingly tall, with dark hair and eyes. She was exceedingly short with reddish blond locks and greenish blue eyes. "I am not Irish! How dare you! I will have you know that every drop of blood in my veins is English! Every drop!"

Aidan scratched his clean-shaven chin. "Odd. I do recall a story…oh, a lovely, romantic story, told by old Katy McGuire about how her great uncle had caught the eye of a particular great grandmother of yours when they were young." His blue eyes twinkled. "How they seemed to have gotten along, too. Seeing as how that story is floating around I'd say it's possible you might be more mutt than English. In fact, my blood may be purer than yours." Aidan's lips spread in that slow, infuriating smile again.

"Mutt?" she screeched. "What impudence!" She stomped her foot and sputtered in an effort to get her enraged thoughts out of her throat. "My family name is Coddington. A good, sound, very English name. Not Irish, and not even a trace of mutt!"

"Or, I suppose it could be on your mother's side."

"Oh!"

"And I do remember you having a taste for potatoes."

Penelope jerked Daisy's reins and started past Aidan, toward the door of the stables. "Really, Aidan, you act as though your station is equal to mine. Your familiarity is more than can be borne at times!" She shook her head. "Whatever could be the matter with you?"

"Ah, Penny. I just wanted to see your pretty eyes light up in fury one last time. I'm leaving the estate this morn, never to come back here again."

Penelope stopped dead in her tracks. A curious blend of emotions swirled inside of her. "What do you mean? Where could you go?"

"Anywhere I choose. The whole world is waiting for me. It's time I made a life for myself. I feel pulled away for some reason. It is time for me to travel."

Penelope turned, knowing surprise shone on her face. Aidan, leaving? But he had always been there. Been there to banter with her and tease her when it seemed that no one else cared even to talk to her. Of course, the possibility of his leaving had always been there. Aidan was not an ordinary servant. He seemed to want more than the others.

"Where will you go?" she asked.

"America. First to Boston, then out west. Mucking out the stalls of other men's horses was never really what I had in mind for myself. I maybe want some horses and stalls of my own to muck. I hear in America even a poor Irish boy can make a good life for himself."

That he would have such aspirations had never occurred to Penelope. Rapidly, she blinked away a sudden wetness in her eyes. Ridiculous! She wouldn't cry over a stable hand!

"I'm a strong man. I'll be making my way just fine. I suppose Ethan or one of the others will ready Daisy beginning tomorrow."

He really did want to leave her here then. Leave her alone with her father's eternal absence, the memory of her dead mother, Horatia's iron hand. Penelope hoped her tears were not visible. "Well then, I wish you luck in your new life."

Aidan stepped forward, clasped her hand in his warm one, and squeezed lightly. "And I wish you luck in yours." When he dropped her hand, she noticed it felt very cold. "You'll be marrying soon, Penny. Don't let your husband doll you all up. Don't let him use you as some bought and paid for mannequin to display his wealth upon. You're more than that. I can see it there, shimmering just beyond all your posturing."

"What do you mean?" She sensed a compliment somewhere inside all that ambiguity. Wasn't that one of the reasons why men took wives, as a way to demonstrate their wealth to the world? She turned her nose up at him. "Really, Aidan, you act as if you have the right to pass judgment on us."

"Don't play the snob with me, Penny. You're not that way. Not really, I remember."

Another half compliment, half insult. She didn't know what to say so she didn't say anything. Daisy stomped and tossed her head beside her, eager to leave the stables. Penelope no longer felt like riding, however. All the joy had been sucked out of the day.

"My mother told me something right before she died," he continued. "I just want you to be careful, all right? No matter what, you fight. I know you can because you're a scrapper, Penny. Under all those silken flounces, you're a fighter with a will of iron."

She frowned. The servants had always said his mother had possessed second sight. Not that Penelope believed in any of that rubbish. "What are you talking about, Aidan? What did your mother tell you about me?"

"She said—" He gave his head a shake. "No. I won't say any more. Don't scowl at me that way, Penny. I'll be leaving you now. Remember what I said, about you being more than frills and expensive lace work," he smiled. "Besides I always thought you looked better natural." With that said, and one last squeeze to her hand, he turned and left the stable.

"Gone," she whispered to herself after he'd left. She stroked Daisy's nose absently. Suddenly the stables, which she had known all her life, seemed oddly cold and foreign.

Aidan strode back through the doors and her heart leapt with a joy that neared pain. "I'm not leaving here without doing something I've been wanting to do for a good few years now," he muttered as he strode toward her.

Before Penelope could react, or even simply draw a breath, Aidan's arms came around her and his lips pressed against hers. His tongue swept into her mouth and mated with hers. She stiffened, and then melted against him. This was not a chaste, safe kiss, like the ones her suitors had given her. It was hot, passionate and unrestrained. This was the kind of kiss she dreamt about.

Amazed, honeyed pleasure licked its way up her spine, leaving a tingling in its wake. God, hadn't this been what she'd always wanted? Wasn't this what she thought about in the dead of night while her hands strayed to parts of her body meant only for her future husband?

He withdrew a little and searched her eyes. She let out a sigh and inhaled his scent—leather and man. He spoke so close to her mouth, his lips brushed hers. "Somebody needs to kiss you right, before you marry one of those half-dead suitors and you never get kissed proper again."

He lowered his head and his smooth lips brushed hers. He kissed her top lip, then her bottom with exquisite care, sending another jolt up her spine. He covered her mouth with his and Penelope kissed him back. His warm tongue slipped between her parted lips and branded the inside of her mouth.

Penelope felt her knees weaken and he held her around her waist, pressing her against the small of her back and tight up against him. The swell of her breasts brushed his hard chest, sending a fast lick of fire shooting through her and making her nipples tighten into hard little points. How good it would feel to have his mouth on them—laving his tongue over them, and finding every little ridge and hollow.

Dropping Daisy's reins from her already lax grip, she wound her arms around his broad shoulders. Her fingers found the hair at his nape and threaded through it. She cursed her gloves, wanting to feel his silky hair against her skin. She wanted to feel every inch of him against her.

Once she'd come upon a couple of the servants in the stables. From the shadows she'd watched them copulate in several different positions. They'd used a wealth of crude words she'd never heard while they went at each other. At the time she'd been both aroused and disgusted. Now Penelope couldn't help but envision Aidan doing the same things to her while they used the same forbidden, naughty words aloud to each other. Just the thought of it made her throb with want.

If anyone came into the stables right now and found them, her reputation would be savaged beyond repair. Strangely, the desire coursing through her blood made her not care in the least.

She dropped her hand to the outside of his pants and rubbed at the hard length of him. "Touch me," she said into his mouth.

He tensed and hesitated at her demand, and then relaxed as though surrendering. Dropping his head, he kissed the swell of her breasts where they bulged from the top of her gown. A gasp of pleasure escaped her throat when he licked the mound of one, as close as he could get to her nipple. Her awareness of her femininity and his masculinity shot up to a near painful level.

He returned to her mouth and spoke against her lips. "You don't know how much I've wanted to touch you, or for how long," he murmured. He kissed her again, his tongue delving in to dance against hers. At the same time, he hitched her skirt up with one hand, keeping the other at the small of her back. He hunted through the complicated folds and layers of her clothing, pulling here and untying there, finding her sex with a practiced ease that gave her pause. He cupped her damp pussy and she held her breath. She'd never been touched so intimately before.

Any thought she might have had on the subject was quickly wiped away at the first brush of his finger against her sex. "You're wet," he growled with audible pleasure into her mouth. He rubbed the callused pad of his finger over her folds and nibbled her bottom lip at the same time.

Penelope gasped and closed her eyes. He stroked over her, rubbing at a particularly sensitive spot, and then slipping his finger within her. Her hands tightened on his shoulders and she whimpered into his mouth as he thrust his thick finger in and out of her. It felt better than anything had in her entire life. She would explode from pleasure if he continued.

His breathing grew ragged and he groaned. "You're so tight, Penny. I want to be inside you," he rasped in a voice thick with desire.

Penelope made a series of unintelligible noises under the onslaught of the magic he was weaving around her pussy. He ground his palm against that sensitive place as he stroked into her.

"You feel so sweet," he murmured close to her ear. "I bet you taste delicious."

Those crude, forbidden words stabbed through her, making her feel wanton and wanted...that combined with his hand working her, caused pleasure to explode over her body and ripple out, overwhelming her. He covered her mouth with his, consuming the sounds of her climax.

The pleasure still tingled through her body when she whispered, "Aidan, please. I want you. I want more. I want you inside me."

"You're drunk with lust, Penny. I've already taken you too far. You don't know what you're saying."

"I do know," she insisted and laid a kiss on his lips.

"No. We can't. I won't ruin you. I'm not—" He brushed his lips over her forehead and she closed her eyes, enjoying the intimate gesture.

"You're not what?" she murmured.

He slipped his hand out of her skirts. A finger brushed her cheek, and the air stirred. Penelope stood, her face tipped up, lips parted, eyes closed as pleasurable, languid shock stole her ability to move.

A dove cooed in the rafters and fluttered its wings. She opened her eyes and he was gone.

* * * * *

The carriage lurched and slammed Gabriel back against his seat. He let out a sigh that blew a tendril of his long black hair away from his face. *Mon Dieu* but humans did not know how to travel comfortably. He closed his eyes as the first wisps of the hunger curled in the pit of his stomach, coalescing into something greater, something less controllable, far too quickly for his taste.

"My, I hope it's not too long before we arrive. I wonder how long a trip it is from Boston to New York. Feels like we've been traveling forever."

Gabriel focused his gaze on the young woman who sat in front of him. Her dress and black cloak were buttoned to her chin against the chill of the day. A fashionable, jaunty hat was firmly set upon her small head of upswept brown hair. "Only about 190 miles as the crow flies."

"Yes, but we are not crows."

Speak for yourself. He wished he'd been able to take animal form for this journey and avoid a lengthy trip by uncomfortable carriage. But he needed to save *sacyr* for now, for he would need much of it to travel between worlds in the coming days.

"I'm Regina," the woman said.

Gabriel reached out and clasped her hand, bringing it to his lips for a kiss. He raised his gaze and watched her brown eyes widen as he flipped her hand at the last moment and allowed his lips to linger on her skin of her wrist, sipping her essence.

"Gabriel," he answered so close to her skin his name brushed her. He could feel the blood pumping through her veins, could hear it surging through her heart. It would be nice to wait until he arrived in New York to feed, but he had a feeling the *sacyr* would not allow him that. Not now. Not when the equinox was so close.

Regina drew her hand away. A curious little smile curved her lips. "Where are you from, may I ask? I hear an accent but cannot place it," she said. Her cheeks were flushed and Gabriel knew his touch had affected her.

Gabriel waved a hand. "Originally, France, but I travel a lot."

"Ah, France! *Je parle un peu le français.*"

The woman prattled on, but Gabriel hardly heard her. He was far too busy controlling the hunger that was little by little growing stronger. Normally, he had excellent control, but the impending equinox threw him off. His body now demanded sustenance even though he'd fed well on the boat coming over from Europe.

Much was afoot. The One was coming. He could feel it in his bones, through his blood. They'd embraced every marked human they could find in order to find him. Time grew short, the equinox drew near, and the danger became great, brewing a supernatural war. The One would arrive soon. Even now the marked poured into New York City, not understanding why, merely called by the rising energies of the coming battle. Indeed, if they did not hear the call, events within their lives would force them to New York, to the Tenderloin District and, finally, to the Sugar Jar and Gabriel.

It was important he get back. Perhaps the One they sought had already arrived.

"Gabriel?" The woman reached out and touched his knee in a flirtatious way. Gabriel fought the growl that threatened to trickle through his lips. "I asked where you'd been born. I am merely trying to pass the time in an amusing way. Forgive me if you think I'm prying."

Gabriel narrowed his eyes at Regina's throat. He knew a warm vein pumped there, under the fold of her cloak. *Non*, the hunger was not being easy with him today. "You seem to want to know all about me, and so I shall tell you. I was born in the year of our lord 1610 in a small village in Bretagne. It is a region of France to the west of Paris."

"1610? But that's imposs—"

"Impossible that I should be 280 years old? I assure you it is not, *mademoiselle*. In fact there are others far older than I."

Regina's eyes widened in alarm and Gabriel almost pitied her…almost. "You are quite mad, sir!"

"You wanted to know about me and so you shall know. As I said, I was born in Bretagne to a poor family. Indeed they could not afford to eat. So, myself, a child of uncommonly good looks, they sold to an artist in Paris when I had but ten years in order to be a model. The artist, his name was Guillaume de Sant, was a lover of men, but not of children." He waved his hand. "He never amounted to anything as a painter. He was a man ahead of his time in that regard, but I digress. But what is wrong, my dear,

Regina? You've grown pale. Are we not passing the time in an *amusing* way?"

Gabriel could hear Monia, his *mère de sang*, even now...*never play with your food*. But it was so much fun!

"Driver, halt!" Regina cried.

"*Non*. You will sit quietly and listen to my tale," Gabriel commanded, using a bit of glamour.

Regina lowered her eyes dutifully. "Do go on."

"Guillaume had a lover named Jacques who took a liking to me. Even though I wanted nothing to do with Jacques, Guillaume grew increasingly jealous. When I turned eighteen, Guillaume told me to leave his house, and so I did. This was not a good time in France. There was much hunger and unrest. I did manage to find work and a place to live and then...I fell in love. I had eight years of happiness with her. When she died I was ruined with grief. I would have joined her in death, I think, had it not been for Madame Monia and her lover, Vaclav."

"Madame Monia?"

"*Oui*. She took me to her *auberge de plaisir*. Um...that is place where the Demi-Vampir can live and feed and be under the protection of the fully Embraced. Like a brothel, you know?"

"Vamp...*Vampir?*" Regina's eyes widened. "Like vampire? Like the creature in the folk tales and penny bloods?"

"*Oui*, that is correct, but you are calm," he commanded. Using glamour on humans was ridiculously easy. Gabriel had run into few able to resist.

"I am calm."

"*Exactement.* Anyway, we are nothing like the creatures depicted in fiction or folklore."

"But—"

"Shh…listen. Demi-Vampir are the unfortunates who are not strong enough to be full Vampir. They feed off sex, pleasure, lust whatever you want to call it. In any case, I was food for the Demi-Vampir for nearly seven years."

"You had sex with half vampiric creatures for nearly seven years?"

Gabriel raised a brow. "But you are quick, Regina. Yes. It was not an unpleasant time. You'd be surprised how much pleasure even a Demi-Vampir can bring you. Of course, it's nothing compared to the pleasure one of the fully Embraced can bring. Humans who lay with a fully Embraced Vampir nearly always become addicted. In any case, one day I fell very sick. Again, I nearly died, but my mistress had grown fond of me and so she Embraced me in order to save my life. I was strong enough to pass through the Demi and attain full Vampir-hood." Gabriel sketched a bow from his sitting position. "And here I am."

Regina merely frowned at him. Gabriel knew well it was all far too much for her human mind to grasp. He sighed. It ruined his fun. "You are tired, Regina."

"I am?"

"*Oui*, very, very tired. You want to sleep now and you will remember none of this conversation upon awakening. *Repetez, s'il vous plait.*"

"I want to sleep now and will remember none of this conversation upon awakening."

"*Oui.*"

Her head dropped and her eyes closed. "Zzzzzzz."

Gabriel rolled his eyes. "Oh, wonderful, she snores." He moved over to sit beside her, his fangs already lengthening. He tipped Regina's head to the side, unbuttoned her cloak, and sank in. He'd sate the *sacyr* now and hope the One would be waiting for him back at the Sugar Jar.

Chapter Two

"Ow!" Penelope glanced down and saw that her maid, Carolyn, had pierced her skin with one of the clasps of her corset. Blood welled and trickled down the plump of a snow-white breast. She looked up and glared at Carolyn making sure lines of displeasure criss-crossed her forehead. "Now look what you've done. It will leave a mark."

Carolyn wiped the blood away with her kerchief. "I'm very sorry, Miss Coddington. I'll try to be gentler."

"See that you are."

Carolyn's fingers found the drawstrings of her corset once more and pulled. Carolyn could not really be blamed for her tense incompetence. The entire household was upset these days.

His death had been just plain odd. How many times had father gone up and down those stairs? Hundreds, thousands of times and never once had she seen him so much as stumble.

Penelope slipped into her mourning gown and allowed Carolyn to fasten the many buttons that ran down her back, and adjust her bustle. She glanced around her bedchamber. Among the rich gilt- and mother-of-pearl-covered furniture, boxes and trunks stood open all over the floor. Gowns, ribbons, and negligees were carefully and lovingly packed within each. Her departure from the Coddington estate, her childhood home and the residence she'd always thought she and her future husband would inherit, was imminent.

Penelope looked out the window in the direction of the stables. Her stomach twisted, then fluttered. She brushed her lips with her fingertips, and then shook her head. Never did she look at the stables and not think of Aidan.

She'd dreamt of him again last night. In the darkest hour, in a place far from here, he'd stripped off every last bit of clothing from her body. She'd done the same to him and had finally seen his beautiful manhood, his cock, as the coarse would say, spring free and stand up hard for her. She'd taken the length of him into her mouth and suckled him until his body tensed, and he'd made sounds of pleasure, throwing back his head and exposing his strong throat. She'd licked him at his very root, drawing him into her mouth and laving over him with her tongue from its plum-shaped tip and down its vein-tracked length.

He'd come hard and long in her mouth and she'd greedily swallowed every last bit of the hot nectar he'd had to give her. But still he'd wanted her. He'd pushed her back and used that beautiful cock on her. He'd spread her legs and stroked into her to the hilt and took her in every position she'd seen the servants in. He'd—

Her cheeks heated and she closed her eyes. She was the most wicked of women to think such thoughts. If Horatia ever knew, she'd be so ashamed of her.

Aidan had said he'd felt called away, that it was time for him to travel. Penelope envied him the ability to act on that impulse. She, too, felt drawn away. Something in her thrilled at the possibility of leaving the constricted life of a well-bred English lady. But such adventures were not in her future. She had responsibilities here, ones she could not shirk.

Carolyn did up the last of the buttons, and Penelope turned, eyeing her reflection critically in the mirror. Her strawberry blonde locks were pulled to the top of her head in a twist. Several long red-gold tendrils had escaped to fall around her face. Large blue-green eyes, slightly puffy from crying, stared back at her. They were set in a face with alabaster skin, high cheekbones, and a chin a bit too pointy and lips too full for her taste. Two weeks ago she'd have made a good marriage. Now, without the illusory promise of her father's money, she had only her beauty to trade on.

Even now, Horatia awaited with news from her father's solicitor, telling her what was left from her father's estate after the creditors had taken their pieces.

Penelope left the room in a rustle of skirts and descended the marble staircase leading to the foyer. At the bottom, tears welled up in her eyes and she said a silent prayer for her father. Last weekend, in the middle of the night, her father had fallen down the stairs and broken his neck. He'd been dead by the time they'd reached him.

She swept into the drawing room with tears rolling down her cheeks and her throat constricted with sorrow.

"Oh, my dear girl! Sit, child," Horatia motioned to a damask covered footstool. Movers walked in and out of the room, each carrying furniture. Penelope let out a sharp breath at the sight.

"The solicitor has been by with…the news." Horatia tried a brave smile, but it trembled.

Penelope sank onto the footstool. Her heart sank right along with her. "The news."

"Oh, my." Horatia sat down beside her and clasped her hands in her own. "We could not have known. No one knew, dear."

Penelope's eyes widened. "What didn't we know, Horatia?"

Horatia heaved a sigh. The corner of her eyes glistened. "Mr. Fitch, the solicitor, has spoken with your father's accountants, and it looks as though there's nothing left, my dear. There is nothing left over for you but a modest, very modest, yearly income."

"Nothing," Penelope gasped, "but a very modest yearly income? How modest is very modest, Horatia?"

"Genteel poverty, my dear."

Penelope gasped again. "Do you mean to say that I am close to destitute?"

"Your father left you little else but debts, Penelope. And you know the money was all his. Your mother's side of the family was not wealthy. Your parents married for love. After she died...I'll be frank...your father sought solace in many different pursuits, sporting women and gambling being the primary two. He was young, his death unexpected. He was very liberal with his money. You know well he was a different sort of man, your father — far too generous with his funds."

"He was free with his money for my benefit, Horatia. You must admit I never wanted for anything material."

"Hmm, yes, that he was, my dear, that he was. However I do believe most of the wardrobe and the personal frivolities of which you speak will need to be sold off to cover your father's bills. I do not mean to be cruel, but it is best you prepare yourself for the inevitable. As well as being very generous, he had too large a love for the gaming halls. He lost nearly all his money to gambling debts. He lost the entire fortune." Horatia waved a hand around the room. "All this was merely a facade."

Two workmen walked past carrying a settee covered in burgundy silk. The room was almost completely raped of furniture. Large clean squares marked the walls where paintings had hung. Dust bunnies caroused in the corners where the servants had neglected their duties, and even the drapes had been removed from the windows. Their voices echoed in the room, making it seem larger and emptier than it was.

"He'd hoped to marry you off to one of your richer suitors," continued Horatia. "But as you've already come to realize, because of the scandal they've...." She trailed off, making a helpless gesture with one hand.

"Who would have known two weeks ago that all of this would come to pass?" Penelope whispered. Two weeks ago her father had been alive and home for the weekend from London. He'd brought her a small porcelain horse. He had been a generous, if not attentive father.

Penelope had done her best to please him, make him love her. But her father had only enough room in his heart for one woman, and Penelope had murdered her long ago. Tears pricked Penelope's eyes afresh.

"And Daisy?" Penelope whispered.

"I'm sorry, child."

Tears coursed down her cheeks not for the loss of her material possessions, but for her father and her lost horse. Would everyone and everything she loved leave her?

"Penelope, you've two relatives in New York. Both are dowager great aunts from your father's side. They still have quite a bit of money and have retained excellent family names."

"I do?" she sniffled.

"Yes. I can't believe your father never spoke of them. Wilhelmina and Therese Pierce—a tenuous link, I realize. Nonetheless, it is all you have at the moment. You must realize that the best chance you have for finding any sort of profitable situation for yourself lies there. I've taken the liberty of sending word to them of your imminent arrival."

Did she have an entree into New York society? Could it be?

"Perhaps you can look forward to a good marriage after all," said Horatia.

Penelope reached out and covered Horatia's hand with her own. "Where will you go?"

Horatia pressed her kerchief to her nose. "I shall go to live with my cousin in Sussex."

Penelope hugged Horatia. "I will miss you." She meant it. Theirs hadn't been the easiest of relationships, but Horatia was the closest thing she had to a mother.

Horatia only sniffled in response.

Penelope pulled away. "What about Daisy? How can I lose her?"

"She will have a good home with her new owner."

Penelope squeezed her eyes shut against a sudden stab of sorrow in her stomach. "When must I leave?"

"Tomorrow. Tonight will be your last night on this estate. In the morning we will put you on a ship bound for Boston. From there, you will take a train to New York. You will travel with but one servant who wishes to go to America. I know it seems soon, and all of this is quite a shock for you. However, these circumstances call for drastic measures, my dear. You will have to take some of your fine note paper, for letters of introduction...."

Penelope stared out the window toward the stables and half listened to Horatia explain what would happen on the morrow. Aidan had left six months ago and she wondered where he was right now. She couldn't help but wish he were here.

When Horatia had finished speaking and taken her leave, Penelope went for a ride. Once she'd ridden Daisy far from the stables, she discarded her saddle, and rode the horse hard and fast bareback. Daisy's hooves hit the ground at a satisfying clip and Penelope let her hair be freed by the wind's wild fingers. She rode Daisy like she never had before, feral and free.

For the first and the last time.

* * * * *

New York

The hansom smelled like someone had stuck a dead chipmunk under the seat. Penelope held her kerchief to her nose and concentrated on the scene outside the window. The oil lamps illumined the colorful clothing of those who passed under their glow. The moonlight bleached the color from the rest of the city.

She examined the city's inhabitants critically in an attempt to identify the pickpockets, beggars, and prostitutes she had heard so much about, but try as she might she could not recognize them.

When the train had pulled into the central station, the cover of heavy darkness had done little to mask the city's grunginess. Tall buildings were pasted like cardboard cutouts against the blue-black sky. The clean country smell of her ancestral home had disappeared somewhere in the middle of the North Atlantic and had been replaced by the odor of soot and sweat after they'd disembarked in Boston and caught the train to New York.

Penelope gripped the handles of her reticule. She wished Horatia had accompanied her, instead of the servant. The boy's sullen demeanor had turned to interest when the ship had sailed into Boston harbor. He'd mumbled something about heading west and had disappeared after they'd docked.

Penelope would be thought of differently now that she was not protected by her father's wealth. She fully realized that up until now she'd been spared the indignities endured by those girls of a reduced circumstance. She touched the money she had pushed deep down inside her reticule. Fifty dollars. It would not get her far.

Penelope had to admit that despite her dire circumstances, a part of her thrilled at the adventure. She enjoyed discovering this strange, new land and having the feeling that she was truly responsible for herself. She supposed a proper lady should be shocked at the turn of events, but then, Penelope had always know she was not a proper lady.

The cab stopped and the driver opened the door. "Number six, Fifty Ninth Street," he said. Penelope climbed out and the driver lifted her bags down for her. A stately brownstone towered above her. On the other side of the street sprawled a large park that reminded her of the Coddington estate in the evening.

The driver set her luggage by the door while Penelope sought the coins to pay. When that was completed, she drew a deep breath, walked up the steps to the door, and rapped twice.

"Pierce?" a clearly annoyed older man in a tasseled sleeping cap said when she asked for Wilhelmina or Therese. "No Pierce here, you've the wrong address. No Pierce in this house."

Hastily, Penelope located the address, written on a piece of white vellum. "But sir, this is the correct...this has to be the residence of—"

"No Pierce here." He closed the door in her face.

"No Pierce?" Her voice sounded hollow in her ears. She turned only to find that the hansom had left. Thinking that Horatia had given her the wrong street address, Penelope went next door. She received a response much like the one she'd already received. Undaunted, she tried the next door, and the next. By the end of the block, she sounded desperate and more than a little crazed.

The last door closed in her face and Penelope sat down hard on one of the steps, the skirts of her simple gray travelling gown swathing her legs. What to do now?

A wind blew, biting through her woolen cloak, and shadows danced on the stairs. Penelope shivered. Apparently something had gone very wrong, but there had to be a way around this ordeal. What she needed now was some sleep and food. A hotel could provide those things, and she could locate a policeman tomorrow. They would surely be able to help her.

Picking up her bags again, she headed down the street. Unfortunately, it was becoming late and most of the hansoms had retired for the evening. Penelope walked for a good hour, knowing neither the city nor the landmarks. She hoped to find a hansom or a hotel…or simply a commercial district where something might be open.

A private carriage rolled down the fog swathed street in front of her, the horse's hooves clip-clopping quickly on the cobblestones. She stepped out into the street and raised her hand, trying to signal it to stop. The coachman snapped the horse's reins, so they increased their pace and the wheels hit a puddle, spraying muddy water all over her coat and face.

Penelope lowered her hand in dejection, wiped the mud from her cheek with the flat of her fingers, picked up her luggage and kept walking.

From time to time she could have sworn she heard someone behind her. The sound of shoes crunching the late fall leaves met her ears. She saw a shadow flit from the corner of her eye. Penelope picked up her pace, uncaring that her luggage was heavy and the handle bit into her hand.

The streets grew darker and darker. Even the moon had hidden itself. Exhausted and cold, Penelope stopped by the entrance of an alley and set her bag down. Tears pricked her eyes. She should be in her great aunt's house now, sipping hot chocolate and telling her relations of her travails. Instead she was on a lonely street in the middle of a strange city searching for a nonexistent hansom. A tear rolled down her cheek, followed by another. She did not deserve such horrid circumstances. She covered her face with her hands and gave into her emotion.

"Are you all right, miss?" came a baritone voice to her left.

Penelope removed her hands and looked at the speaker. A large, grizzled-faced man stood looking at her with concern. "No," she sobbed. "I'm lost. I'm cold.

I can't find a hansom, and my luggage is too heavy for me to carry. Can you help me, sir?"

He nodded and a glint of silver caught her eye. She looked down and gasped. In one thick hand, he held a knife. "I can help you a little, miss. I'll relieve you of your luggage and your reticule." His teeth flashed white in the darkness. "It'll not be so heavy for ye' then."

Penelope opened her mouth to scream but shock and fear snatched her voice away. She watched in horror as the man gathered her luggage and reticule and disappeared down the alley.

* * * * *

Aidan stood in the hallway of the Sugar Jar and stared. He should be disgusted, but arousal tightened his body instead. A woman knelt on the floor and took a man's thick cock into her mouth. Her dress had slipped down her shoulders, revealing glimpses of creamy white breasts and rosy erect nipples. She sucked and laved the man's organ with obvious rapture, bringing it far down her throat and drawing sounds and rude murmurings of pleasure from her client.

Further down a nude woman sat on the edge of a table. Another woman knelt before her exposed pussy, hungrily licking her and stroking a long, thick object, shaped like a cock, in and out of her pussy. The woman was braced back against the table, the long line of her neck exposed in rapture.

He'd never seen such things in his life. When he'd entered the brothel, he'd expected to find wanton acts, but he'd never expected to see them openly displayed. Aidan's cock hardened as he walked forward. The manager's office was at the end of the hallway.

A woman who leaned in a doorway stepped out and pressed him against the wall. Her hand strayed to his shaft, and she rubbed it from outside of his pants. "Veeerrry big boy," she whispered. "Let me tasssste you," she hissed. She smiled, showing small pointed teeth.

Aidan pushed her away. "I have business here and it isn't with you."

Aidan hadn't had sex in a long time, not since before he'd held Penny in his arms back in England. Penny was the one he wanted, not any of the other women who'd flaunted their bodies at him since he'd been in America. He knew he had to get over her soon.

But that seemed to be an impossible thing to do.

He made his way down the hallway. If he didn't need the money, he'd leave right now. When he arrived at the end of the corridor, he didn't bother knocking. He opened the manager's door and set his bag down in front of the desk with a thump. "I'll be straight with you, Mr….?"

The man sat forward in his chair, his long black hair shadowing a face with dark blue eyes and a strong cleft chin. He folded his hands in front of him, took a deep breath, and closed his eyes. After a moment he opened them. "*You* may call me Gabriel," he said in a complex accent. French was perhaps beneath it all.

"All right, Mr. Gabriel—"

"Just Gabriel."

Aidan frowned. "Gabriel...I heard that you're one of the only places that will hire Irish and that you're looking for bodyguards for your...uh...establishment. I'm strong. I'm a hard worker and I'll protect your girls with every ounce of my will. But I'm not planning to stay around here long. I'm going west just as soon as I can raise enough money to do it."

"And will you protect our men? We have those here too."

"Uh...and your men," Aidan replied.

Gabriel raised an eyebrow. "Not afraid of men who like men, are you?"

Aidan steadied his gaze. "No. But my desires don't go in that direction."

"Ah, good. I am not drawn to men either, but I am not afraid of those who are. I believe all well-adjusted men are not."

Gabriel's gaze flicked over him, taking him in from head to toe dispassionately. He rose and came around the desk. Aidan fought the urge to back away. There was something about this man that felt different and it was unsettling. Gabriel walked to him and put his hands on Aidan's shoulders.

"Hmmm...interesting. You are indeed very strong. One of the strongest I've ever come across. The arrivals are becoming stronger closer to the equinox," Gabriel said under his breath.

"What do you mean?"

Gabriel backed away from him and turned toward his desk. "Tell me, Aidan—"

"How did you know my—"

Gabriel turned. "Shush. Listen carefully now. Tell me. Was there anything interesting about your birth, Aidan? Anything out of the ordinary?"

He'd been born with a black caul. His mother had said it made him different. "What does that have to do with my finding a job here as bodyguard? And how do you know my name when I never told you?"

Gabriel raised an eyebrow. "Not very good at taking orders are you? How did you service a wealthy English family with an attitude like that?"

Aidan fisted his hands and eyed the door at the side of the opulently decorated room. He stood his ground. "How did you know that about me?"

"Aidan, I know a lot about you. I even know why you happen to find yourself here at a brothel in the Tenderloin District of New York City, when you meant to be clear to the middle of the country by now. America is not all you thought it would be, is it?"

It hadn't been. Aidan had never expected to find people here so hostile to immigrants. He'd arrived to a sea of hatred and calls of "*Mick, go home.*" It had been a rough trip and now he was out of money. He couldn't make it west as he'd hoped. Not yet, at least.

"Maybe so," Aidan admitted. "But that doesn't explain how you know so much about me."

"I know you were born special, Aidan. Born for a purpose that you don't even understand yet. It is by no accident you found yourself here. You who were born *marked.*"

Aidan picked up his bag and headed for the door. "You're insane," he muttered under his breath to calm the beating of his heart. His mother had said as much to him when he'd been young. Born with a caul. Born marked. The same thing she'd said of Penelope. "*The evil ones will be looking for you and her both,*" she'd vowed.

"People keep telling me I'm insane," Gabriel mused behind him. The door slammed shut in front of Aidan aided by no one. Aidan stopped dead in his tracks.

Gabriel put a hand on his shoulder and Aidan reacted. He dropped his bag, whirled, caught Gabriel by the throat and pushed him against the wall. "I don't know what you are, or how you know so much about me. All I know is you're letting me walk out of here *now.*"

Gabriel laughed through his constricted throat. "You and I are far more alike than you realize. You just don't know it yet." He placed his hands on Aidan's forearms and with incredible, mind-numbing strength pulled Aidan's hands away from his throat. Aidan yelled in rage as Gabriel forced him to the floor.

"What I have to do now won't hurt a bit, *mon ami*." Gabriel's eyes glowed with a white light, and a warm tingling started in Aidan's belly and spread outward. He gasped as it engulfed his body. White light clouded his vision and images flooded his mind.

A strange, dark force consumed him, burned away all vestiges of his past, wiped away any last bit of innocence he'd possessed. Immense, shimmering knowledge replaced it as foreign as the stars above and familiar as the earth beneath his feet. An absolute and total darkness touched just a whisper of his soul. It stole his breath, his thought, all of his emotion. It was coming. This evil was coming soon; ready to consume the world as he knew it. Ready to consume all of life. It had to be stopped and the only way to do it....

Aidan swore under his breath. The light faded away, the tingling warmth receded. Aidan found himself curled up on the floor. He opened his eyes to stare at Gabriel's polished black boots. "Oh my God," he whispered.

Gabriel held out his hand. "Rise, *mon ami*. Such a one as you should not be upon the floor. You were not prepared. I shocked you. Please forgive me, but I saw no other way. You are incredibly strong and I thought I might lose you before I could trigger your mark."

Aidan grasped his hand and stood. Fever raged through his head. He couldn't see clearly. He blinked his eyes to clear them and the room swam.

"*Mon ami, mon ami....*" Gabriel's voice came from somewhere far away. "We must get you to Monia. There is only a little time after the mark has been triggered to Embrace you. I would do it, but it is sexual in nature. We've already established that I don't swing that way and neither do you."

Aidan knew what Gabriel meant to do—make him Vampir. He'd been marked for it since birth. He didn't know how he knew that, but he did. "No," Aidan muttered. He went for the door, tripped and fell to the floor.

Gabriel pulled him to his feet. Aidan tried to focus on his face, but couldn't. "You must be Embraced, Aidan. Once the mark has been triggered, there is no turning back. If you don't allow Monia to Embrace you now, you will be Demi-Vampir, feeding always from sex. Come!"

"No!" Aidan roared. He pushed Gabriel away with strength to match the Vampir's and raced out the door. He stumbled down the hallway, causing the whores to squeal and back away from him, and lurched down the stairs and out into the street. The early morning sunlight hit him hard, making his already burning body scorch.

He made his way into a nearby alley, where it was blessedly dark, and sank to the ground. So this was what it was to be marked. This is what his mother had talked about so many years before. Aidan closed his eyes and shivered violently while at the same time he burned with fever. Perspiration ran down his forehead. Thank God Penelope was safe in England. Thank God.

Time compressed, then expanded. Shapes in the alley swam in his vision. He blinked, trying to focus on one thing.

Then the world went crystal clear. He could see everything—every individual crack in the wall of the building in front of him, every speck of dirt that lay within. He could read the tiny text printed on the crumpled and rain-dampened paper swirling around his feet.

He could hear too, every whisper of the wind on the gravel-strewn ground, every single shining voice of the people who passed on the street beyond the mouth of the alley.

Aidan looked up. A beautiful woman with long, black hair stood over him. Her exquisite body was clad in a sleek silk nightgown. Dark nipples showed through the material.

She held out a slim, elegant hand. "My name is Monia. I am Gabriel's *mere de sang* and I will be yours as well."

Mere de sang…blood mother…. He didn't how he knew that. He didn't speak French. "No," Aidan gasped. But he had no strength to try and get away.

"*Bel homme*, you cannot escape this. You were born to it." She knelt beside him and placed her hands on his chest. "Even now the mark consumes you. If you are not Embraced soon, you will be a Demi-Vampir for all eternity and that would be a waste for a man as strong as you. You could the One, *bel homme*. Humanity needs you to take your place among us. It is your right and your responsibility."

She placed a hand to his temple and closed her eyes. Aidan felt her mind sweep against his and then go deeper as she probed it for memories. He tossed his head back and forth, but he couldn't stop the invasion.

"Your mother was wrong about us, Aidan," Monia purred. "She had the sight, it is true, but she was raised on the false folklore of our kind. Your mother believed the Vampir to be an unnatural evil. We are not. She confused us with another force in this world. This will be explained to you soon."

Aidan braced his hands on the pavement beneath him. Small stones cut into his palms as he tried to force himself up. "No. My mother was not wrong."

"Hush, *bel homme*. You think of someone. You think of…a woman." Shimmering enveloped her form. "You think of this woman." Monia's long black hair shortened a little, became thinner, and changed to a strawberry blond color. Her eyes morphed to a blue-green and her body and face became Penelope's.

"Penelope," Aidan breathed. "But you aren't my Penny."

"No." Monia smiled. There was knowledge in her eyes of a kind Penny hadn't known yet. "But this will help you come to me and my Embrace, *non?* Time is wasting. The opportunity the triggering of your mark has afforded you will not last forever."

She drew him into her arms. "Come to me, Aidan," Monia said in Penelope's voice. "You know I've always wanted you. Remember what you were thinking in the stables? That you're not good enough for me? You *are* good enough. Our class difference doesn't matter. I want only you...only you. I love you, Aidan."

Aidan's fevered mind worked. How long had he dreamed of hearing those words issue from Penny's lips? "Penelope," he choked out. Desire started low in his stomach and spread to his cock. God, how he wanted her.

"Yes." Penelope/Monia opened her mouth and Aidan watched her canines lengthen into fangs. "Let me Embrace you, my love," she purred.

She tipped his head to the side and lowered her mouth to his flesh. Sharp fangs broke his skin and he gasped. His hands gripped her shoulders. There was a pain at first, sharp and sweet at the same time, but it faded quickly to pleasure as she drew blood from his throat. His cock hardened and orgasmic bliss consumed him. He groaned.

Aidan writhed on the ground. His hands strayed to Penelope/Monia's waist, moved to her breasts. He wanted to spread her legs and bury himself inside her. Lust bowed his spine, made him roar in anguish.

Monia released him and rocked back on her heels, forcibly separating his hands from her body. She looked once again like herself. His blood coated her fangs and dripped down her chin. She lifted a brow. "You are a heady vintage, *bel homme*. Spicy and strong. I will not perform the Embrace fully because you love another, as do I." She smiled ruefully. "You and I both will simply have to stay aroused." She brought her wrist up and bit it, and then lowered it to his mouth.

Lust tightened his body in a vise. He wanted to rut like a stag in mating season. Images of Penelope danced through his mind. How she'd look clothed only by the moonlight, by only his own, broad hands.

He reached out and drew Monia to him. He needed to find ease. The pressure on his groin was unbearable. The only thing that stopped him was the blood. He wanted that more than sex. Dark, thick blood dripped from the wound she'd made. He licked at it and found it tasted better than anything he'd consumed before. He curled his hands around her forearm and latched his mouth to her wrist and sucked.

The blood flowed into him, suffusing his body with something new, something strange, changing him, and improving him. He felt every single part of his body dying, yet being reborn at the same time. He could feel every single pebble beneath him, could hear Monia's breathing, her heart pumping. He could hear the mice scrambling along the side of the alley. He could smell the street, the humans who walked there. He could smell their very blood.

Darkness clouded his vision and he let go of Monia's wrist. Falling back against the wall he closed his eyes and let go of his awareness.

"Sleep, *bel homme*, and awake rejuvenated," Monia whispered. "Awake reborn to the world of Vampir."

Penelope....

Chapter Three

Penelope….

Aidan's voice breathing through her mind woke her. "Aidan?" she murmured.

She roused a little, but did not open her eyes. Her mind reviewed recent events and she grimaced. "All a dream," she mumbled. "All just a horrible dream." The housekeeper would come soon to bring her morning chocolate. A stable hand would be readying Daisy for her morning ride even now.

A sharp wind gusted and chilled her. She woke fully with a start and surveyed the dirty alley she'd finally fallen asleep in that morning.

She shook her head as if to clear it and rubbed her gritty eyes with dirty hands. It was only wishful thinking that Aidan would be anywhere near her. Chances were he was somewhere in Kentucky by now. Maybe he even had his beloved stables running at this very moment.

Her stomach growled and Penelope put her palm flat against it. Hunger gnawed at her from within. She needed to find food, but at the moment she couldn't force herself to move. Despair had sapped all the will from her body. Her father was dead. She had no money, nor any family or friends to rely on.

She was completely and profoundly alone. She had only herself now.

The cold slowly crept into her muscles and she watched as a few flakes of snow fell. She stayed that way for a long time, thinking of nothing but the falling snow. Eventually, a mouse crawled onto the hem of her coat. Penelope gave a full-throated scream, sprung to her feet, and bolted from the alley.

Once out onto the street, she blinked against the morning light and surveyed her surroundings. Carriages clattered down the road, passing well-dressed men and women who walked down the sidewalks, stopping now and again to gaze at the beautiful items on display in the shop windows. She appeared to be in a wealthy part of town. At least there was that.

"Move along, vagrant! You damn Irish, come over here and then live on the streets taking charity from the good citizens of this country." A tall, well-muscled man, whom Penelope believed must be the proprietor of a nearby shop came at her, shaking his fist. "Your kind isn't welcome in this part of town. Move along before I call a policeman."

Penelope stiffened her spine and swung around to face him. "I am *not* Irish."

The man stopped short, apparently surprised she'd dared speak back to him. "Listen, lady. I don't care what you are. Just move along."

"Can't you hear the educated English accent I have?" she asked, exasperated.

The man's face turned an interesting shade of purple and he took a few menacing steps toward her. "All I hear is an accent, immigrant. Now move! You're scaring away business."

Penelope hesitated, wanting to argue further.

He raised a fist at her and shook it. "I'll cuff you one if don't get out of here *now!*"

He looked serious. With one final expression of defiance, she turned and walked down the street.

People stared at her as she passed and Penelope tried to keep her chin up and gaze straight ahead. They would not make a member of the Coddington family feel like a common street person. She pulled her coat closed and walked on.

Her nose led her to a bakery where several different kinds of muffins and biscuits were displayed in the front window. Her stomach growled in response to the smell. The light lunch she'd had on the train yesterday had long since worn off. But it wasn't the food that had her peering into the window. It was her reflection.

Her hair had come out of its tight coif and now hung in untidy tendrils around her face. Deep, dark circles marred the creaminess of the skin beneath her eyes, distorting her age and beauty. Mud stained her serviceable, modest looking traveling gown. She spat on her fingers and rubbed a smear of it from her cheek. "No one will help me and I'll freeze," she whispered to herself. "I'll freeze or starve to death on these streets."

She stared at herself in the window and let the words hang in the air between herself and her reflection. Aidan's words came back to her. *No matter what, you fight. I know you can because you're a scrapper, Penny. Under all those silken flounces, you're a fighter with a will of iron.*

"No," she whispered. "I won't give up."

She stood looking at herself in the window for a moment, shivering a bit in the breeze, then pulled the hood of her coat over her head and stuffed her cold hands deep into the pockets.

And pulled out a couple of bills.

She stared down at the money that lay in her palm. Two whole dollars. Never had she been so happy to see such a pitiful amount of money in her life. She remembered now that she put the change there before leaving the train station, and had meant to replace the bills into her reticule. Two dollars meant hot food; it meant lodgings, at least for a while. Suddenly Penelope had a plan. She could find a room to rent and send word to Horatia explaining her plight. Perhaps Horatia could send her the correct address of her great aunts.

In the window, Penelope watched a street vendor's reflection as he pushed his cart along the sidewalk behind her. "Fish," the hawker cried, "Fresh fish! Sold for a song! Make you strong and liiive long!"

That message spurred her legs into motion. In order for her to think clearly, she needed sustenance.

Across from the bakery was a small cafe. She went in and found a table in the back, next to the stove. She ordered a hot breakfast of ham, eggs, and a cup of hot tea. When she was finished she felt stronger and better able to meet what lay ahead of her optimistically.

Back out on the street, Penelope asked for directions to the nearest district of boarding houses and headed off in that direction. A new hope beat in her chest.

At the corner of two busy streets, she saw a well-built man with dark brown hair climbing into a hansom. The way he moved was so familiar.... "Aidan!" she cried, running toward the cab. "Aidan!"

The cab rolled past her with the curtains drawn. She shook her head, dismay and heartache welling up within her. So stupid...of course that hadn't been Aidan. Aidan was far from here. She had to get him out of her mind. She had to concentrate on her survival now.

She raised her head and spotted a boarding house across the street. She walked to it and pushed the heavy front door open.

Approaching the wrinkled man behind the desk, she flashed her best, prettiest smile. "I've come to inquire about renting a room."

The old man looked her up and down and sneered. "We don't rent to your type. Go down to Five Points, or the Tenderloin, they'll take ya there." He turned back to the newspaper he'd been reading.

She set a hand to her hip. "My type?"

He turned from his paper and fixed her with a steely stare. "We don't rent hourly, honey."

Indignation mixed with shame tightened low in her stomach. She forced it down and summoned Coddington icy steel into her voice. Anger would get her nowhere, haughtiness might. "I do not wish to rent *hourly*, sir. I wish to rent a room to occupy for as long as I can afford."

He leered her with rheumy eyes. "Gonna do business in it? If so, I want a cut."

She drew a breath and shook her head. "You have a misconceived notion about me, sir."

He clucked his tongue. "Pretty lady, alone. Obviously down on her luck. I don't have the wrong notion about you. If you're not sportin' now, you will be soon." He flicked the edge of his paper straight. "Three dollars a week, payable immediately."

She sighed. "Do you rent for a shorter duration than that?"

"No, miss. A week. That's as short as we allow." He gave her a pointed look. "Keeps out the driftin' riff-raff, you know."

"I can't afford that."

"Like I said, Five Points or the Tenderloin's better for the likes of you."

Penelope turned and walked out the door.

Seven more establishments, seven more dead-ends. Penelope pushed open the door to exit what had been her last hope. They'd turned her away just as all the others had. Her feet were heavy and her stomach was growling as she crossed the street and began walking south. The sky was growing dark and a chill wind had picked up. Penelope could smell snow in the air. She tucked the collar flaps of her coat around her throat, but it did little to cut the cold.

Facing the possibility of another night on the street, Penelope had to seriously consider the clerks' mention of Five Points or the Tenderloin District. Thus far, she had tried to stay away from those areas. However, every passing referral had sent her closer to the more poverty stricken parts of the city. The houses in the area she was currently in had began to look somewhat more rundown, but they were by no means dilapidated. She was sure she couldn't be in the Tenderloin yet, although she knew she wasn't far from it.

The snow was coming down in heavy, fat flakes now. It would pretty, she thought, if she didn't have to sleep on it. She lowered her head and let a tear drop onto the snow covered ground. It was the first she'd shed since her nightmare had begun. She'd been in such a state of shock before. None of what had been happening to her had seemed real. However with the severe lack of sleep she was being subjected to and the revelation that she could actually die before morning did much to wake her from her shocked numbness.

She counted five more teardrops before she lifted her head and saw the small fire in the alley off the street she stood on. Three people were gathered around it. Vagrants, she assumed. A fire would keep her warm through the night and keep her from death. If they would allow her presence at it.

Before walking over to them, she extracted her money from her pocket and put it down her boot. She wasn't going to take any more chances. As she walked toward the three figures around the fire, she reviewed the things Aidan had taught her so long ago. The most sensitive places on a man were his groin, eyes and nose. If she ever had to defend herself, Aidan had said to go for those areas.

"Whad' d'ye want? If ye come lookin' fer a piece o' this fire, you'll be disappointed," said an impossibly old woman when she approached.

"Matilda, what's it to you if we have an extra body at our fire?" answered a man, whose face was concealed by a voluminous scarf. He turned toward Penelope. "Do you need a place to spend the night?" His voice sounded cultured, his accent educated.

Penelope approached them slowly, her hands held toward the seductive warmth. "Yes. You don't mind?"

"Yes, we do."

"No, we don't," the man said, throwing a chilling glance at the old woman. She looked down and away from Penelope guiltily.

Another man shifted by the wall. His face and neck were completely covered by a wrap.

The man standing at the fire indicated him. "That's Michael, he doesn't talk much. I'm Charlie, and that's Granny Hobbs. Just ignore her."

Granny Hobbs made a raspberry.

"I'm Penelope," she said, throwing Granny Hobbs an apprehensive glance.

Penelope settled on a piece of ground where the snow had all melted, and curled into a ball, sighing as she absorbed the warmth of the fire. Charlie sat down next to her. Penelope registered the indecency of all this somewhere in the back of her mind. But since yesterday, all notions of what was proper had ceased to be important.

"What brings you to the street, Penelope? Your accent is upper class English. You're obviously green, considering the way you just came up to us. You probably come from a good home. Am I right?" he asked.

"I came looking for relatives, but they weren't there. Got the wrong address I think. All my money...stolen. All my luggage." She yawned. Her exhaustion was taking her over she didn't know how much longer she could fight to stay awake....

"Did you try the post? They've got a directory of everyone in New York."

The post! Of course! Why hadn't she thought of that before? She mumbled her thanks before slipping off into sleep.

* * * * *

The day dawned brutally cold. Penelope opened her eyes and got up, trying to work the chill out of her bones. The fire was still raging. Each member of the motley group had awoken in shifts to feed it. Penelope herself had been up twice, throwing in handfuls of paper and chunks of wood. She realized the gravity of the situation. If the fire were to go out, their sleep may have very well turned into a sleep of death.

Stomping her feet on the ground, she looked down at Charlie. He lay on his left side and the wrap around his face had come loose. Thick black hair slightly shadowed a face that was utterly charming. He had thick black eyelashes, long as a girl's and a finely sculpted face. A slight growth of beard covered his strong chin, but that only seemed to enhance his attractiveness.

He opened one chocolate colored eye. Then he shifted and sat up, exposing the other side of his face to her view. Discolored and misshapen flesh marked him from the crown of his head and down his neck on the right side. Penelope gasped.

"I'm sorry, I should've warned you." He held out a hand as though entreating her not to run away.

"No, of course not. I'm so rude. Forgive me, please. It's just that—"

"Aye, he'd be a bonny gent, wouldn't he, gel? If 'e didn't have that mask o' horror on one side o' his face," Granny Hobbs broke in, just slightly left of tactful.

Penelope shot the chilling look this time. She tried to marshal her mouth but the question passed her lips before she could stop it. "What happened?"

"I was born this way. I come from a home undoubtedly every bit as prestigious as yours. I'm sure you've heard of the Scythchildes?"

Penelope's mouth dropped open at the name of one of Boston's richest families. She'd heard of them clear across the Atlantic.

"My father could not bear to have someone as ill-favored as I carrying his blood, especially not his first-born son. He couldn't look at me at all without shivering in revulsion. So, he sent me off to an institution. My mother desperately wanted me home and so sneaked me there when I was around six. I lived in the mansion in secret until I was fifteen and my father discovered me. He disinherited me and tossed me out on my ear. Ever since then, I've been trying to earn my own keep. However, there are not many who will hire me to do much of anything. I tend to scare people and make their children cry."

"Oh," Penelope said, at a loss for words.

The shrill sound of a whistle pierced the air and a policeman, waving a billy club came running into the alley. Charlie scrambled to his feet. "Run!" Penelope didn't have to be told, she did it involuntarily. The policeman looked like he wasn't afraid to use his club.

"Whad' d'ye doing? Let me be!" cried Granny Hobbs.

Penelope looked back and saw the policeman struggling with her. She was outraged that the policeman would accost an old lady, one who down on her luck anyway. She flew at him. Penelope pummeled the officer's back. "Let her go! She's old and helpless!"

The policeman turned and with one hard smack across her face sent Penelope to the ground. The policeman freed Granny Hobbs and came toward her, his baton held loosely in one meaty hand.

"What's a purty thing like you doin' out here on the street?" he asked. Dark possibility glimmered in the depths of his black pupils. "Need any help, little girl? I could get warm food in your belly and give you a warm place to lay your head."

Penelope laid a palm to her sore cheek. In his bed, probably.

The policeman knelt and took her by the upper arm. Her gaze locked with his. "Come on now, girl. I don't take no for an answer." His grip tightened painfully and she knew he'd leave a bruise.

Anger blossomed low in her stomach and spread out. She kicked up, feeling the crunch of the man's genitals against her booted toes. The policeman keened in pain, put both hands to his crotch and bent over double. A stream of obscenities spewed from his mouth.

Charlie stood behind him holding a thick piece of wood. He bashed it over the policeman's head and he went down like a sack filled with lead.

Charlie tossed the wood aside and held out his hand. "C'mon there will be others where he came from." She took it and he pulled her up.

"Damn gel, ye nearly 'ad me killed!" shrieked the old woman. "Old and 'elpless, am I? I'll no longer spend any time wi' the likes o' you! Cost me a night in a warm place and food in my belly, ye did." She turned and stalked off.

"Ungrateful," Charlie muttered.

Together they made their way out of the alley. Delicately, she held a hand to the cheek that the policeman had hit. She had to get out this place. She had to find her great-aunts.

"The post," said Penelope. "Please bring me to the post."

At the post, the employees looked as though they would rather throw them out than aid them. She had a bruise blooming like a hideous flower on her cheek and he with his deformity. Instead, they helped her quickly, leafing through the pages of the directory with speed.

There was no record of a Wilhelmina or Theresa Pierce in the entire city.

"Check again," Penelope demanded.

The woman checked again. Again, no luck.

Penelope left the post with her heart heavy. Charlie followed her. She didn't say a word as she walked down the street. Every last bit of hope had been tore from her.

With a thump she sat down on the stoop of one the brownstones next to the post. Charlie sat down beside her. "Alone," she said. "I never knew what that word really meant until now."

Charlie was silent. "You have no other family in England you can summon, no friends?"

"Honestly, we have no family. My parents were both only children and my grandparents are long since deceased. Yes, I have relatives, but they are very far removed. And anyway I do not have their addresses. As far as friends.... We were so isolated in the country. I did take part in society, but it was not on a regular basis. My mother died when I was young and my father was absent most of the time. He did not concern himself overmuch with my social activities. I have no close friends to which to turn. I did have suitors—"

"I'll bet."

Penelope gave him a sharp look. "I had suitors, but they fled once the promise of money was gone and the scandal of my father's gambling problem came out." She made a scoffing sound. "Which tells you what they truly thought of me."

Eventually, hunger as their motivation, they got up and began to walk down the street.

For several blocks they walked, Charlie educating her on all the different ways to scavenge for food and Penelope grimacing at each of them.

Charlie rounded on her. "Penelope, you don't comprehend the seriousness of your predicament. You have no choices available to you. You scavenge, or die. The situation is bad for me, very dire. For you, an attractive young woman, it's far worse. You have nowhere to go for shelter, my dear. Do you understand that? You are too old for an orphanage, not ill or crazy enough for Bellevue, and the alms houses…."

Her spine straightened. "I would sooner freeze on the street than take charity or go to an alms house."

"Well, isn't that wonderful logic? Mark me, when you start to freeze, you'll change that haughty little mind of yours quick enough. They'll have no place for you, in any case. It's winter and you've come late to underworld of poverty. There will be no more beds. Soon, you'll be wishing, just like Granny Hobbs, for a place in the prison for the night."

She had a torrent of words poised on her tongue, and she was just getting ready to let them fly when she spied a sign.

Winder's Hotel
Affordable Rates

Mr. Winder was an overweight man with a heavy beard and mustache. He informed her at the desk that the rate was one dollar and fifty cents a week, and there would be no "guests." If there were, he was entitled to a percentage of her profits.

Penelope had been outraged so many times in the last few days that she barely blinked at this newest insult. There would be no "*guests,*" she assured him. Mr. Winder had looked a trifle disappointed at that.

"May I see the room?" she asked.

He looked at her slantwise. "Nope, no time. You either want the room, or you don't. Got a lot of folk here in the Tenderloin that will take the room."

So she was in the infamous Tenderloin, the play land of the depraved and destitute. Penelope blinked. Fine. So be it. How bad could the room be? In any case, it had to be better than the street. Scowling, she pushed her dollar and fifty cents, the rest of her money, across the desk to him, and he pushed a key back.

"It's on the fourth floor," he mumbled at her before returning to his newspaper.

"Well, good luck to you," Charlie said when she came back outside and told him she could afford to stay there, at least for a week.

"Keep warm," she told him. "Thank you for everything you did. Thank you for the policeman."

"Watch out, all right, Penelope?" he said as he was walking away.

Penelope watched him walk down the street, his scarf covering the deformed part of his face. Silently, she warred with herself. He'd helped to save her life back there in the alley. She should call him back, offer him a warm place to sleep for the next week, at least for tonight.

But how could she share a room with a man she hardly knew?

How could you sleep outside on the filthy ground? How could you attack an officer of the law? How could you scavenge for food like a homeless mongrel?

She opened her mouth to call him back, but Charlie was already gone. He'd turned a corner and disappeared into an alley. Penelope turned and headed back into the hotel.

Winder's was gloomy at best in the downstairs lobby, but as she mounted the stairs to the fourth floor, it became frightening. Candles mounted on the walls lit her progress. The place didn't even have electricity. In the places where there weren't any candles, it was black as pitch. In those dark spaces, she gripped the banister with increasing terror. The air was filled with creaks, squeaks and rustlings that had a distinct rodent like quality. She could hear the thump of footsteps, muffled voices and occasionally the sound of muted laughter, or low, sick sounding moans.

There were no candles to light the fourth floor, just the wan daytime glow leaking in from the grimy window at the far end of the hallway. She had to feel her way down the hall using the wall. Just as she had found her door and had placed the key in the lock, she saw something move out of the corner of her eye. Slowly, she turned her head. There in the corner, a black, misshapen heap moved. Two eyes gleamed at her from above the folds of a grungy scarf.

Too surprised even to move, Penelope watched as the thing flopped over, made a low moaning sound, and then rose to its feet. With a slow shuffling motion, the thing moved down the hall toward her. Penelope looked away, fearing the thing was coming for her and began turning the key in the lock desperately.

It wouldn't open.

With every passing second, the thing grew nearer and Penelope tried harder to get the door open. When the thing was finally behind her, she closed her eyes and prepared to die.

"You gotta jiggle it," came the thing's voice, a rough and scratching sound. It passed her and went down the stairs.

Penelope's eyes popped open and she jiggled the key in the lock twice. It gave and she flew into the room, slamming and locking the door behind her. She went straight to the window, before she'd even had a chance to inspect her surroundings, and threw it open.

"Charlie!" she screamed.

* * * * *

Aidan sat on the edge of Gabriel's desk. Gabriel stood with his back to him, looking out the window.

"Hmmm...I wonder who Charlie is," Gabriel murmured. "Ah, that must be the man in question."

Aidan stood and walked to the window. "What are you talking about?"

"Look there, *mon ami*. I suppose that's Charlie, charging to the damsel's rescue like a knight of old. I do hope he's duly rewarded for his effort."

Aidan pushed aside the cream colored curtain and watched a man running down the street and into Winder's hotel, his long black overcoat flapping out behind him. He looked to the window where Gabriel's attention had been focused only to see a flash of reddish-blond hair—a color so familiar it made his heart ache—and the filthy curtains fall shut.

"You've gone pale," said Gabriel.

Aidan turned away from the window. "I'm fine." Just yesterday he could've sworn he'd heard Penelope call his name as he climbed into a hansom. *Christ*. He was losing his mind.

"Missing someone?" Monia's smooth voice greeted them as she stepped into the room.

Aidan looked up and watched her cross the Persian carpeted floor. When he'd awoken after Monia had embraced him the entire world had been different, larger and stranger—far more dangerous. Although his mark had shielded his mind from the worst of the shock of being Embraced. It had been as though a part of him had always known one day this would happen and accepted it as the inevitable…as fate…*like coming home.*

His heart still twisted when he thought of what he'd lost. Though, truthfully, he'd never *lost* Penelope at all because he'd never had her. She was far too good for the likes of him. But Aidan couldn't deny that somewhere in the back of his mind he'd nursed the fantasy that maybe he'd make good in America. Make it so good that he would've been able to return to England and whisk Penelope away with him. That was even more impossible now than it ever had been.

Dreams. Curse them.

"I'm fine," Aidan repeated, pressing the palm of his hand to his eye in an effort to reduce the severity of the oncoming headache.

Monia eyed him with her beautiful, mysterious, knowing dark orbs. She walked across the room, her skirts swishing against her long legs. Running a finger over Gabriel's desktop, she murmured, "I'm also missing someone."

"Vaclav has left for Boston?" asked Gabriel.

"Yes. He left this morning. After so many centuries together, you'd think we'd want some time apart." She flicked a glance at Aidan. "But love can be so unreasonable and powerful sometimes, defying all common sense...even class boundaries." She turned her beautifully formed body toward him. "But *mon bel homme* knows all about that, doesn't he?"

"Sometimes love can be cruel, yes," Aidan answered.

Gabriel sat down in the chair behind his desk and tented his fingers on the ink blotter in front of him. "You have fed today, Aidan?"

"Monia took me out and showed me how to use glamour to befuddle the mind of a woman. I took blood from her and left her with a pleasant memory." Feeling the woman's warm life's essence pump into him had been better than sex, but not better than feeling Penny's wanting body pressed up against his.

"You have powers other than the glamour, you know," commented Monia. "You are able to compel humans to do as you wish, and can communicate via telepathy. You are able to shape shift, and you have the power to travel through the dimension just to the side of ours."

Aidan's gaze snapped up. "What do you mean?"

"You can travel through dreams," said Gabriel. "Like the Dominion, you are able to enter any human's awareness while they dream. Any human you wish to contact."

Possibilities ruffled through Aidan's mind. "Really."

"Ah, *oui*. Now, normally these abilities do not show themselves to an Embraced until they are far, far older than you. However, you have demonstrated that you are quite the exception. You are unusually strong. I believe you might indeed be The One we have been searching for so long. You are manifesting as a very old Embraced. It will be interesting to see what you will be like in a century from now. You have already shown us that you can control the *sacyr* and use glamour. I feel certain you'll quickly master our other abilities, as well. Even dream travel. You will be able to contact whomever you choose, wherever they may be."

"Should you desire it, of course," came Monia's teasing voice. She knew how tempted he would be to find Penelope within her dreams. Any contact at all would be heaven.

A knock sounded on the door. It opened and a man stepped through. He was tall, broad of shoulder and narrow of waist. Long brown hair hung free to the middle of his back. Dark eyes regarded him from a handsome face with olive skin. An unusually large brown and gold tabby cat followed him in and sat down beside him. "It is always nice to meet brethren," the man said. "I welcome you to our family." A slight Italian accent flavored his words, covered over by a mélange of other accents. Aidan wondered if he would one day sound like that—accent confused by centuries of living in foreign countries. It was more than odd to think he'd live for centuries now...forever, in fact, or at least until he was killed.

"Aidan, meet Niccolo," said Gabriel. "He is also of Monia's line. He is...sort of a vampiric policeman, called an executioner. If one of us neglects the *sacyr*, or is deprived from feeding it for too long, and goes into bloodlust, Niccolo hunts them down and...disposes of them. Can't have members of the Vampir running around killing humans, now can we?" Gabriel flashed a smile. "It's bad Vampir-human relations. He also keeps those Vampir in line that genuinely desire to wreak havoc on mankind. There are many of them out there. They give the rest of us a bad name."

Aidan nodded at Niccolo. He looked strong and something in his dark eyes screamed no mercy. No, he wouldn't like to be on this man's bad side. "Nice to meet you, Niccolo." His eyes flicked down to the cat. The fat cat seemed at odds with this man's personality. A lion or jaguar seemed better suited. "Yours?"

Niccolo laughed, a scratchy, unused sound. "Kara is no one's but her own. She chooses to travel with me, however, yes."

Aidan raised an eyebrow. "Are you saying she's a vampire cat?"

"After a fashion, though she takes no blood. Kara is a familiar…my familiar. She's immortal, like a Vampir, and seems to feed from me somehow. She speaks to me within my mind."

"Some Vampir have familiars," Gabriel broke in. He shrugged. "Some never find theirs, others do. I have not found mine yet and may never. Just as some Vampir have bonded mates. Monia found hers in Vaclav."

Monia stepped to Aidan's side and stroked his hand. "Niccolo will take you now to further your training, *bel homme*. He is going to teach you to shape shift. We have deemed you ready to learn."

"Shape shift?" Doubt curled through his stomach. *So much, so fast.* Not even his mark could stave off all the shock. He nodded his head. "All right."

"Later," Monia whispered. "You and I will discuss how to travel through dreams, *oui?*"

Aidan couldn't wait to learn that.

Chapter Four

Aidan threaded his fingers through her hair, kissing along the line of her throat. His breath was hot against her skin. Her corseted breasts brushed against his hard, bare chest while he sought her mouth. His hands found the buttons of her dress, popping each of them off, one-by-one.

She was warm, safe...loved. She never wanted to leave Aidan's arms again. She belonged right here....

Finally her bare skin was soft and slick against his. He parted her thighs with his knee and slid his cock into her while they stood. Slowly....so slowly he thrust into her over and over until she was crying out, gripping his shoulders for support. Pleasure washed over her, consumed her.....

Penelope awoke to hard, cold reality. Her breath showed in the frigid room and her stomach cramped with hunger. She curled herself under the thin scrap of a blanket, squeezed her eyes shut and wished to have her dream back. Aidan's arms had been so warm and strong around her. His lips had felt so right on hers. His cock had felt so perfect moving within her. Her thoughts drifted back to that day in the stables. Teardrops filled her eyes and squeezed out the corners. She missed England. She missed the estate. She missed Horatia.

But most of all, she missed Aidan.

She sat up and pulled the dusty, cracked hand-held mirror off the bedside table and stared at her reflection. Dark circles marred the skin beneath her eyes. Her cheeks were sunken, her hair dirty and stringy, and her eyes dull.

The door slammed open. The mirror slipped from her fingers and crashed to the floor, shattering. Seven years bad luck. Penelope didn't even blink.

Charlie walked across the floor and dumped two old potatoes and a hunk of moldy bread on the mattress beside her.

Penelope threw the blanket over her head. For the week since they'd checked into Winder's, they'd only been able to find things such as this to eat.

"Come on, Penelope. You can't play the little princess when you're starving. You have to eat and this is all there is. I don't like it any better than you do."

She pushed the blanket away. "We must leave Winder's this morning."

Charlie pushed a potato at her. "I know. That's why you need to eat as much as you can now."

She eyed the potato with distaste and her stomach growled loudly in spite of herself. She picked it up and bit. The cold, pasty, slightly decayed taste of it filled her mouth, and she chewed and swallowed.

"There's a good girl. Penelope...who's Aidan?"

Just hearing his name spoken aloud cause her to nearly choked on the foul potato. "Aidan?"

"Every night for the past week you've thrashed in bed and called out his name." Charlie looked down and played with the edge of the blanket. "Sometimes you moan out his name."

Her cheeks heated. "Umm…Aidan," she said carefully, "is a friend of mine from England." Horatia would wash her mouth out with soap for calling an Irish stable hand a friend.

"Was he a suitor of yours?"

"No. He was a merely a friend. A good friend." She took another bite of potato and chewed. She barely noticed the foul taste now that her thoughts were on Aidan. Every night for the past week she'd had dream after dream of him. Sometimes they made love, sometimes he just held her close. It was the only thing that had made the last week bearable.

After they ate, they got their few belongings together and walked to the door. They shuffled past the lump of a man with the gritty voice who was huddled in the corner. Penelope didn't bat an eyelash. She'd become accustomed to his presence.

Cold, hard air slapped her face when they exited the hotel. Penelope trudged through an inch of snow behind Charlie. He'd said he knew a good place to stay, against the outer wall of a restaurant that was warmed by ovens.

Every step was torture for Penelope after having the safety of the hotel. The wind lashed at her cheeks and she pulled her coat around her tighter. She felt dirty and worthless. All she wanted in the whole world was to lie down on the street and drift to sleep...forever.

"Hey you! Vagrants!" A familiar voice called from behind them. Charlie and Penelope turned to see the policeman that had accosted them the week before bearing down on them, his churning legs kicking up snow.

"Run!" said Charlie.

Frightened into new desire for survival, Penelope did just that. She picked up her skirts and ran. They veered into an alleyway and raced along it. The cries of the policeman echoed behind them. Penelope threw her meager belongings to the ground to gain more speed and desperately tried to see in front of her as the flopping hood of her coat and the glare of the sun on the snow took turns blinding her.

In front of her, Charlie stopped short and Penelope slammed into his back. "Oh, no," he breathed.

Penelope peered around him and saw a brick wall. "We're trapped," she said in resignation, her fingers curling into his coat.

Footsteps crunching on the newly fallen snow sounded behind them. Penelope turned to see the policeman bearing down on them with a raised billy club. He swung it and Penelope dodged it by a breath. It connected solidly with Charlie's stomach and he grunted.

She screamed, watching Charlie fall to his knees holding his gut. The policeman raised his club and she grabbed the end of it, trying to wrench it from the policeman's steely grip. He pushed her hard to the side, slamming her into the alley's wall. Her head connected with a solid crack and she slid down into the snow, barely hanging onto awareness.

She looked up and locked gazes with Charlie. "Run," he rasped.

The policeman raised his club and brought down against the side of Charlie's head with a sickening thud. He fell to the snow-covered ground.

Bile rose up from Penelope's stomach at the sight of her friend lying prone on the ground. His blood stained the snow bright red.

The policeman grabbed her and flipped her to her stomach, pressing his knee into the small of her back. She flailed in the snow, cold seeping into her clothing.

"Ain't gonna nail my balls this time, bitch."

She heard the jangle of metal as he took something from his pocket. It had to be handcuffs. In terror and desperation, she twisted and fought him. "I got lucky last time," she spat in rage. "Your balls are so small it's a miracle I hit them at all."

Penelope cried out in pain as he wrenched her wrists around to her back. "Ah, now that's a misconception. I'll show you how big my balls are just as soon as I get you alone. I'm gonna make you suck 'em." He fastened the handcuffs around her wrists, got off her, and hauled her to her feet. He smiled, revealing rotten teeth. "I always get my woman. Remember that."

Other policeman came pounding down the alleyway. "See to that one," barked the officer, jerking his head in Charlie's direction. "I'm taking this vagrant in with me for disorderly conduct and loitering."

"More unruly micks, huh?" asked one of the other officers.

"They're everywhere," replied the policeman. She watched the officers tend Charlie as the policeman hoisted her over his shoulder and walked back down the alleyway.

Penelope yelled in outrage and struggled. "I'm not giving up to you, you bastard. I'll bite your balls off! I swear I will!"

He clamped her flailing legs tight against his chest. "I'm gonna beat you till you can't see straight, girl. You won't have any strength but to lick and suck me nice after I'm through wi' you. Nah…you and I are going to have ourselves a bit of fun today, aren't we, darling?" The policeman caressed her ass with one idle hand.

Rage flared within Penelope at his words. She struggled; kicking out while his hand was on her rear. She landed a good kick to his stomach that made him grunt. He released her and she slithered off him to land flat on her ass, her handcuffed hands at the small of her back.

"You little...." He came at her and she rolled to the side. He cursed and came toward her, his ugly faced twisted in hatred. She'd never survive this man's treatment. She felt it in her gut.

A shadow figure descended...*descended?* Penelope blinked. Yes, a figure *descended* into the alley and came up behind her abductor.

"How about you have a little fun with me, instead?" asked the man. Without hesitation, the stranger took the policeman by his hair, wrenched his head to the side and bit him.

Everything went a little south of too much for Penelope and her world went black.

* * * * *

Niccolo slammed the door open and strode into the room with a bundle in his arms. Gabriel looked up from the paperwork on his desk to watch him. Across the room, by the roaring fire, Aidan and Monia spoke in hushed tones. They ceased their conversation and watched Niccolo.

Niccolo laid the bundle in the center of the floor. "I found this young woman in an alley half frozen to death. She's in bad shape, starved, and dehydrated. She is strong-willed and also very strongly marked. A police officer held bad intent for her." Niccolo flashed a white, feral smile in the darkened room. "He won't be bothering her or anyone else anymore."

Gabriel crossed the carpet and knelt beside the young woman. Between two fingers he rubbed a tendril of her dusty hair and found a magnificent red-gold. Her eyes fluttered open and flashed a warning at him. He laughed. This one was strong all right. "You'll be happy, Aidan," he said. "She must be Irish with this hair and eye color."

"I am *not* Irish," she rasped.

"Penny?" Aidan asked.

"Aidan," she gasped. Her eyes fluttered shut and she lost consciousness.

Aidan walked over and knelt beside her. A series of emotions crossed over his face like fast moving clouds, leaving shock in their wake. "How can it be?" He gathered her into his arms and stood. "She's mine, Gabriel. I will take care of her." His eyes held a challenge.

"Are you ready for that responsibility, *bel homme?*" Monia asked from across the room. "You are a brand new Vampir. Albeit an exceptionally strong one, but new all the same."

Aidan's eyes flashed. "Mine," he practically growled.

Gabriel shared a knowing look with Niccolo. "Fine, *mon ami*. She is yours. But you do not know yet how to trigger her mark or Embrace her. Will you at least allow our counsel?"

Aidan's arms tightened around her. "I won't allow her to be Embraced."

Niccolo took a step toward him, and Aidan backed away. Gabriel held out a hand to stop both of them. "*Non*. We are all friends here. We are all on the same side, yes?"

Aidan merely stared at him.

"You need to become used to the change you've undergone, Aidan. That takes some time. I remember that well even though it was a long time ago. Unfortunately, time is not a luxury we are afforded. The equinox grows ever nearer as do the Dominion. We have many people counting on us."

"I understand that. And I accept my place within the ranks of Vampir more easily than you believe. But I don't want Penny involved in this. I don't want her endangered."

Niccolo stepped forward. "You are a still a young pup, Aidan, even if you are exceptionally strong. You cannot feel how powerful a mark she bears. It is stronger than even yours. It is the strongest I have ever felt, and I have lived many years. I am older than Gabriel."

"She was born with a red caul," said Aidan.

Gabriel raised an eyebrow. "A red caul? Indeed." That meant much and everyone in the room knew it, including Aidan. Only the very strongest were marked with red cauls at birth. "She must be

Embraced, Aidan. Deep down, because of the knowledge your mark gave you, you know this."

His arms tightened around her and he glanced down at her face. "No." His refusal didn't sound as sure as it had been a moment before.

"It is her destiny. Do you truly think it is so terrible? To become stronger, become impervious to disease, to the passage of time." Gabriel licked his lips before speaking the next. Here was his power card. "You know, Aidan, that if Penelope is Embraced, she will be an equal to you. There will be no more class separation between you. You will both be part of Monia's ancient and distinguished line. You will both belong to our family and can leave the human world, with all its ridiculous social classes and rules, behind if you choose. Everything between you will be possible in our world."

"I won't Embrace her for selfish reasons."

Niccolo cleared his throat. Gabriel watched Kara wind her way around Niccolo's legs and look up at him with love in her green eyes. "Then do it because she could be the One," said Niccolo. "Do it because, possibly, she might be the key in defeating the Dominion on the equinox." Niccolo picked Kara up and stroked her head. "Much counts upon our success."

Aidan backed toward the door. "I'm taking her to my chambers. I will nurse her back to health."

"Fine, Aidan," said Gabriel. "Take her. I will come to see you later this evening after we have fed. Shall we bring a morsel back for you? You cannot feed upon Penelope, you know. She is far too weak."

Aidan gave his dark head a hard shake. "I wouldn't."

"Controlling your hunger can be more difficult than you might think, even for the old ones. Even for one as strong as yourself. Remember, lust for blood can feel like sexual lust."

"I'll manage." He disappeared out the door.

* * * * *

Aidan smoothed Penny's dirty hair back from her forehead. What could have brought to her New York and put her in such dire circumstances? Was it the coming equinox? Was it her mark calling her home to her people? Aidan shivered, surprised at how quickly he was thinking like a Vampir. It had been more than simple to fall into their ways. It had been second nature to him—like a part of him he'd forgotten and recently remembered.

He fingered her silk-like hair. If it had been the call, she'd resisted. Hard.

Her eyelids fluttered open and she gasped in pain. He procured some laudanum and mixed a little for her to drink. He slipped a hand under her neck and put the cup to her lips. She drank it down without protest. Her eyes were wide as she looked up at him. He set the cup aside. He'd already dressed the nasty gash on the back of her head. There was a bruise on her face that was fading, and her hair was matted with dried blood that Aidan was trying very hard to ignore.

"What—"

He set a finger to her lips. "Shh…you're tired and wish to sleep."

The little bit of glamour worked easily on her. Her eyelids fluttered shut and her body went limp. Aidan didn't enjoy deceiving her mind, but it was for her own good. Her body needed rest to repair itself.

She slept for many long hours and Aidan, deep in thought, watched her the entire time. For the most part, it was a deep, dreamless sleep he'd set her into. But once in a while she'd rouse a little, nearing consciousness, and toss her head back and forth on the pillow. Aidan stroked her grimy hair back away from her beautiful face that had grown far too thin for his liking.

"Charlie," she moaned in her laudanum- and glamour-drenched sleep.

Aidan stilled his hand. Charlie? Who was Charlie? Jealousy flashed through him. Maybe she'd come here with a fiancée…or a husband. He fished her hand out from beneath the blanket and saw she wore no ring, but it could've easily been stolen through all the tribulations she'd obviously encountered.

Realization shot through him with a jolt. Oh, yes. *Charlie.* The same man who'd raced to a damsel's distress call. That had been her he'd seen in the window across the street at Winder's. That meant she'd been right under his nose for a week. That meant likely that *had* been her calling his name on the street that day.

That also meant she'd spent seven nights alone in a hotel room with a man named Charlie.

She moaned and tossed her head back and forth on her pillow. He'd worry about who Charlie was later. Right now he needed to concentrate on her. She required food, a bath, clean clothes, and sleep…lots of healing sleep. She also needed to be checked for wounds. She had the gash on the back of her head and that bruise on one cheekbone, but what other injuries did she have? He could see nothing else outwardly. The voluminous clothing she wore made inspection impossible.

Aidan stood and pushed a hand through his hair in frustration. She would hate him if he undressed her, but he didn't trust any of the others with her. He could not ask a female Demi-Vampir for obvious reasons, and he did not trust any of the female Embraced either. He did not know any of them well enough to trust they would not sample her sex or her blood. It was difficult enough for himself to resist with those fine, blue veins running so close, so visible under the delicate, pale white skin of her throat.

Aidan shuddered.

Fine. It was for her health that he removed those vermin infested clothes and checked her for wounds.

If she hated him for it, she did. He'd rather see her alive and hating him than dead of some wound he couldn't see to treat.

His rooms consisted of a bedroom, a sitting room, and bathroom, all connected by a short hallway. He walked to the bathroom and turned on the tap, then asked a Demi-Vampir servant to bring fresh clothing and hot food. Hopefully the bath would revive her enough to allow her to eat something.

Gently, he lifted her up and removed her coat. He laid her on her stomach, her head turned to the side. He started at the top button at the back of her gown and worked his way down.

The Demi-Vampir delivered clothing, complete with nightgown, wrap, dress, corset, stockings and boots. Aidan laid the nightgown and wrap on the back of the chair by the bathtub, shut off the spigot and resumed undressing her.

She roused and shifted on the bed. His hands stilled. "Aidan?" she asked sleepily.

She tried to push herself up and he helped her. "What are you doing?"

"You have to be checked for wounds, and you need to get out of these filthy rags."

She put a hand to her forehead and groaned. "I feel terrible. My head hurts."

His hands fisted. He could not force the anger from his voice. "Someone knocked you around. Do you remember?"

She swallowed hard and licked her cracked bottom lip. "Yes. A policeman."

"He's been punished. He won't hurt you or anyone else again." Steel threaded his voice. He wished Niccolo hadn't been the one to punish the man. Aidan wished he'd been there. He'd have done more than simply drain him of blood. "I'll give you more laudanum for the pain. It's worn off."

She shook her head. Her hand went to her stomach. "No. I don't have any wounds, Aidan, just bruises. I can heal without the laudanum. I want to be able to think clearly." She looked up at him, her eyes shining with tears. "It's so good to see you," she whispered. She reached up and wrapped her arms around him in a hug.

He let his arms wrap around her body. She'd grown so thin she felt breakable. His face came into contact with her throat and he could hear and smell the sweet blood that coursed through her veins. God, it smelled good. *Just one little....*

He pushed away from her, causing her to sway on the edge of the bed and steady herself. "You have a lot to tell me, Penny. I want to know everything. How you came to America and became destitute. Why a policeman in a back alley of the Tenderloin beat you up. But first, you need to bathe and most definitely to eat. How steady are you? Can I help you undress for a bath?"

She looked up sharply. "I may have plummeted a bit on social standing within the last couple of weeks,

Aidan." She raised her chin. "But I still will not allow a man to help me bathe. I still have standards of propriety."

"I don't trust anyone else here to help you. It's myself, or no one."

"Aidan, remember the day you left, what we did in the stables?"

"How could I forget?"

She looked up at him, her blue-green eyes sheened with doubt, fear and desire. "I haven't forgotten either. That's why you can't help me to undress. I…I might forget myself."

They locked gazes. Memories tumbled through his mind, as he knew they tumbled through hers. Heat sparked and arched between them. He remembered what he'd done to her in her dreams. How he'd teased her body until she'd keened for him. How he'd drank from the center of her, laving at her bud and slipping his finger in and out of her until she trembled and shattered under his hands. She wanted him as much as he wanted her. The knowledge tightened his body, made his cock harden. He wanted to make those events *real*.

"Anyway, I'm filthy. Too filthy for you to touch." Penelope broke eye contact, looked away and drew a steadying breath. Carefully, she stood. "I'll be fine, Aidan. If you can find me some clothing, I can bathe myself."

"Are you sure?"

She nodded. "Completely."

"Clean clothing is hanging over the back of a chair by the bathtub. I will be in the sitting room just off the bathroom. But know that if I think you need my help, I'll be there."

Penelope merely scowled at him.

Aidan shook his head. "You're still my Penny, aren't you?"

"Perhaps…but *you've* changed," she accused.

Aidan mouth broke into a grin. "Oh, Penny, if only you knew how much."

She didn't even crack a smile. She simply tipped her head to the side and regarded him. "You're darker now…different. Deeper in some way I can't put my finger on. What's happened to you?"

Aidan's grin faded and he gazed back at her with intensity. He reached out, placed his hand to the side of her face, and rubbed his thumb back and forth over her lower lip. He didn't want to answer her question. Didn't know how to explain it to her. How could she ever believe what had happened to him?

"You're so beautiful," he murmured.

She blushed under the filth and looked down and away. "Not now I'm not. I'm dirty, skinny, and bedraggled."

He forced her gaze to his. "You're always beautiful, Penelope. No matter what."

She looked down as though uncomfortable, and then shifted her gaze to the hallway.

He stepped to the side. "Go take your bath and then come into the sitting room to eat."

* * * * *

Penelope sat in the water until her fingers were puckered and then climbed out, dried herself, and slipped into the nightgown and wrap that had been laid out for her. She brushed the material with her fingers. It was a fine garment, well made. After the week she'd had, changing out of her traveling dress felt like heaven. The clothing was clearly made for a prostitute. Its thin material hugged every curve and hollow of her body.

Penelope searched through a dressing table at the far end of the lushly decorated room and found some toothpowder and a comb for her hair. A fire burned in a small hearth beside the gold and gilt piece of furniture. One thing could certainly be said, the Sugar Jar was a finely decorated haven in the middle of the coarse Tenderloin District. Penelope wondered who was in charge here.

After she used the toothpowder, she squeezed out the excess moisture in her hair and worked the comb through the tangled length as she walked to the sitting room. Aidan stood when he saw her and ushered her into a chair. He took the comb from her, and set a plate of food in front of her. She forgot about everything except that for a time.

Penelope sopped up the sauce from the plate with a piece of bread. "Aren't you going to eat anything?"

"I'm not…uh…."

She looked up to find him staring intensely at her. His gaze was focused somewhere near her throat. "What's wrong?"

He looked away. "Nothing. I'm not hungry right now, that's all."

She shrugged. "You look hungry," she said and then popped the last bit of bread into her mouth. She sat back in her chair, enjoying the feel of a full belly. She felt so much better, better than she'd felt in the last two weeks. "Tell me how you came to be here, Aidan. I thought you'd be clear to Kentucky by now."

He looked back at her and narrowed his eyes. "You first, Penny."

"All right." She told him of her father's death and her lost great-aunts. She told him about having her bags stolen, being homeless, and the evil policeman. "I've had an eventful time," she finished.

"So have I." He pushed a hand through his hair and sank down into the chair opposite her. "So, you're not married."

"No," she said carefully. "And I probably never will be. I have no prospects now."

"Who is Charlie?"

Her hand flew to her mouth. "Charlie!" Images of the blood staining the snow, Charlie collapsing to the ground, flashed through her mind. "After the policeman…." she trailed off. So much had happened between then and now. She'd almost died. Horror speared through her as she realized Charlie might not have avoided that fate. "I have to try and find him. He helped me so much."

"Do you know where you are right now, Penny?"

"The Tenderloin District. In a house of ill repute. Having dinner with a stable hand after being accosted by a policeman like a common street-dwelling lout. If Horatia had any idea--"

"I'm not a stable hand anymore."

She looked at him. "So what are you, Aidan? A bodyguard to whores?"

He hesitated for a moment and then came off his chair. He paced the floor twice like a caged animal and then knelt in front of her, placing his strong hands to her thighs. "I wish it were that simple."

His dark blue eyes were intense and passionate. The heat of his hands bled through the material of her wrap and nightgown. Having him so near made her aware of just how little the clothing covered. The memories of how he'd possessed her body in the stables and in her dreams flooded her mind and tightened her nipples. "Why...why...." she started, her voice a mere agonized, breathless whisper. She cleared her throat, swallowed hard, and began again. "Why isn't it that simple?"

His gaze traveled down her body and back up, lingering at her breasts, her exposed collarbones and the curve of her neck. "This place is much more than it seems, and you are not safe here. You, Penelope, are prey in this place. You're like an antelope surrounded by wolves. The only place you'll be able to stay is here, in my room." His hands traveled an inch up her thighs, dangerously close to her mound. His thumbs could almost brush the hair that covered it. "Can I ask you something, Penny?"

She licked her lips and tried to calm her breathing. His hands on her made all kinds of strange things happen. Her pussy swelled and grew damp. Her clit pulsed and demanded attention. She wanted him to touch her more. "What?"

His thumb smoothed the silk material of her wrap and nightgown over her swollen clit. He did it casually, as though it was normal, as though she was his to do with as he pleased. "Do you trust me?"

She closed her eyes, fighting the urge to spread her thighs for him, and nodded.

Air brushed her flushed cheeks and she opened her eyes. He stood with his back to her, his hands clenched at his sides. "You shouldn't." His voice had gone hard and cold.

Penelope stood and went to him. She smoothed her hands across his back and he flinched. She wanted to encircle him with her arms, lay her cheek against his back, and breathe in the scent of him. Instead she backed away and stood by the table.

"When we were children I wanted to spend every minute I could with you, remember?" she asked. "I thought you knew all the secrets of the universe. I felt drawn to you for some reason I never understood and that draw continued for years. In fact, it never stopped. I just got better at resisting it. Out of all the people in my life, you were the one who was always there for me. You seemed to always have time for me. Even when I was being a spoiled bratling, still you bantered with me, teased me into a better mood. I feel safe with you. Why shouldn't I trust you, Aidan?"

He turned and pierced her with his intense blue gaze. "Because I'm not the same man you knew on the Coddington Estate."

She felt the truth of that radiating out from him in some barely tangible way. She shifted uncomfortably under his heated gaze. It moved from her feet to her head, caressing every inch of her along the way. He took a step toward her and she resisted the urge to take a step back. But this was Aidan. He would never hurt her.

He stopped a breath's space from her.

She looked up at him. "What are you thinking about, Aidan?"

"I'm thinking about what happened between us in the stables, about how good you felt under my hands and mouth. I'm thinking about how good you look right now in that sleeping gown and how much better you would look out of it. I'm thinking about how much I want to tumble you onto the bed, spread your legs and lick you until you keen in pleasure."

Her stomach fluttered at his words. She wanted him, too, but.... "This can't happen, Aidan. I can't succumb to you again like I did in the stables. I'm a nice woman, a respectable woman. Well, I'm trying to be a respectable woman, at least. I have societal expectations to answer to. As soon as I find my great-aunts, life will return to normal, and I can't—"

He took her hand in his and bought it to his mouth. Gently, he kissed each finger in turn, his tongue flicking out to lick at each tip. All the time, his darkened, dangerous gaze held hers. It stopped the flow of her words. She felt her breath catch in her throat. "Come closer," he whispered.

She stepped forward, closing the short distance between them without hesitation. It felt right. Being close to Aidan felt as natural as breathing.

He put his hands on her waist and pulled her up flush against him. His erect cock pressed against her stomach. "You don't understand that none of that matters now. Not a bit of it. The world is so much bigger than that."

He dipped his head and rubbed his lips over hers. Her breath left her again and before she had time to recover it, his hands grasped the edges of her wrap and slipped it over her shoulders. She felt it slither down her body to pool around her feet, leaving her clad in only the revealing nightgown.

Desire coursed through her, warm and languid. It did nothing for her nipples, however. They tightened as though they were cold. She swallowed hard.

Aidan took a step backward and let his gaze rove her body. His eyes flashed dangerously and a muscle in his jaw locked as if he was holding himself back, but it was taking its toll.

"Aidan?" she asked uncertainly.

He reached out and cupped a breast in one hand. He ran his thumb back and forth over the distended tip. "God, the things I want to do to you," he murmured.

She let a small sound escape her throat, and he was there, holding her close around her waist with one arm, his lips covering hers. His tongue delved in and mated with hers. He left enough space between their bodies to let his other hand rove. Everywhere he touched her, he left a trail of fire. He caressed one breast and then the other. His fingers skimmed her lower belly, her buttocks, and her mound. She gasped at the sudden influx of new sensation.

"God," Aidan sworn under his breathe. "Dear God." He stepped back, grasped the sides of her nightdress and pulled it up. It slipped over her head like a sigh and fluttered to the ground beside them, leaving her skin warmed only by the light of the candles, the oil lamps scattered around the room, and the heat they generated between their bodies.

His action shocked her, but aroused her at the same time. He pulled her up against the hard heat of his body and the fabric of his shirt brushed her breasts. She shivered with desire, feeling her pussy stir with longing and become slick. She wanted to know what it felt like to have a man between her legs. She wanted to know how Aidan's cock tasted.

She'd do anything right now to find out, even give up her reputation by surrendering her virginity before marriage. Penelope realized then just how powerful lust could be.

He touched her shoulder, letting his fingertips graze her skin. He caressed her throat, rubbing in circles with his thumbs, and then went lower, exploring her collarbones and the hollow between them. Her heart rate sped faster every degree further his hands dropped. He trailed down and cupped her breasts. Her nipples hardened into tight little peaks against his palms and her breath came faster.

He caressed her nipples with his fingertips before going to his knees in front of her and bringing his hands to the small of her back, then sliding lower to cup her buttocks. He laid a kiss just above her belly button, and then dragged his lips down over her heated flesh, letting his tongue delve in to taste her navel before heading south. He squeezed her buttocks as he kissed her mound. Her hands tightened on his shoulders and she let out a quick breath.

He lowered his mouth further still. Using his thumbs, he pulled apart the delicate flesh sheathing her clit and kissed the very top of her pussy. His tongue stole out and licked the pleasure point he'd stimulated so skillfully in the stables. Penelope couldn't stop the low moan that escaped her lips.

He didn't linger there. Instead, he went down further still, scattering kisses on her upper thighs, her calves and finally tasting the tender, sensitive flesh behind her kneecaps.

Penelope was a mass of burning want by the time he was through. He stood and she noted the hooded, dangerous look in his eyes. It seemed to say that he wasn't done and by the time he was, she'd be well and thoroughly fucked.

"Stop me now, Penny, because soon there'll be no going back," he said.

She lowered her eyes in a sudden fit of nerves, and then thought about all she'd been through in the last week. She'd met the cruel underbelly of life. She'd almost died doing it. Those experiences changed her point of view—her priorities. Couldn't she have something she wanted just this once? Couldn't she allow herself to find solace and caring in this man's arms? She wanted that. She needed it.

She looked back up at him, her gaze steady—challenging even. With that look she gave her nonverbal assent to the question he asked with his vibrant blue eyes and smooth, dark voice.

Their gazes locked...literally. Penelope's jaw went slack as she stared into his eyes. Lust shone there and something more...something deeper, alien and primal. White light flashed through them. A breeze of information blew through her mind, quickly transforming into a tornado. His eyes flashed and something in her stomach exploded and spread out. It rolled over her, consuming her, burning her.

Her eyes closed and her knees gave out, collapsing her like a rag doll.

Chapter Five

She felt strong arms catch and hold her before she hit the ground. She heard Aidan's voice speaking urgently to her, but he sounded so far away. Penelope was too busy dealing with the knowledge that slammed into her, tearing away everything she thought she knew about her life, her very world, and replacing it with a terrible, dark wisdom — that of the past, present and future.

Something dark loomed on the horizon of reality. Every breath they took brought it closer. It was an evil that consumed everything in its path. Only one thing could stop it....

"No," she moaned. She flailed her arms as if to ward it off, but it was in her mind, nothing physical that could be battled. She felt herself being lifted and then laid on something soft. Hands touched her forehead, ran through her hair. Someone rocked her back and forth and Penelope fought her way back using these tactile sensations as anchors.

Her eyelids fluttered open to reveal Aidan. "I didn't mean to trigger it," he said.

Her teeth chattered. She felt cold and hot at the same time. Her mind felt folded under a hundred cotton blankets. Knowledge that tore every last shred of her innocence swirled through her, mixing and melding with the person she used to be. Indeed, she was not the person she'd been only minutes before. Something Aidan had done had shifted reality on its axis.

"Trigger?" she managed to push out.

"Your mark."

Her mark. The knowledge flowed through her. She'd been marked at birth. The red caul had been the physical representation of the internal difference between herself and humans. She'd been marked to one day be Embraced as Vampir. Part of her was shocked and disbelieving. Another part was relieved to be finally coming home.

Someone knocked on the door and Aidan called for them to enter. The fact that she was stark naked registered somewhere deep within her, but didn't seem to matter much. She shivered against Aidan and his arms tightened around her.

Footsteps sounded on the wood floor, growing nearer and nearer the bed. A male voice hummed in disapproval. "Everyone in the Sugar Jar felt the trigger, Aidan. There was far too much lust between you two for it not to happen. It was like putting a flame near a powder keg."

"I must Embrace her," answered Aidan.

"You have no choice, now." He sounded pleased. "Do you know how?"

He paused, drew a breath. "Yes. I won't lose her to the Demi."

Penelope opened her eyes to perfectly crisp and clear sight. She could feel every fiber of the blanket she lay upon and became explicitly aware of Aidan's body pressed up against her. Lust unfurled in her lower stomach and spread out. She whimpered and ground her hips down into the mattress.

Gabriel cleared his throat. "I will leave, mon ami, and give you two privacy. I will be but a thought away, should you require my aid." Penelope heard his footsteps as he crossed the room and the door close.

She looked up at Aidan and desire swept over her so hard it bowed her spine. This flood of lust made what she'd felt before he'd triggered her mark look like a trickle. She needed him within her. She needed his cock now. The whole house could be coming down around their ears and it wouldn't change the fact that she needed him inside her.

Now.

She sat up and moved over him, pushing him down on the bed beneath her. "Aidan," she said, running her hands over his muscled chest, his shoulders and his hard, flat stomach. "I have wanted you since I was old enough to notice. Since I was old enough to realize what a male and female could do to each other with their bodies. I want to taste you, Aidan. Now."

Her fingers found the edge of his shirt and pushed under it. She found his nipples and ran her fingertips over them teasingly. "Penny, I—" he started. She ground her hips, rubbing her naked pussy along the hard length of his cock. Only the thin material of his pants separated them. Her action stilled his words and he groaned. "It's the trigger talking, " he finished.

"It's not the trigger. I wanted you long before this. I used to fantasize about you at night while I touched myself. I used to bring myself to pleasure, imagining you were the one doing it."

He groaned. "This is too much. I can't take this and still stay a gentleman."

The muscles of his stomach rippled when she brushed her fingertips across it. Her hands went to his pants and undid them. "I don't want you to be a gentleman, Aidan."

She reached down and pulled off his shoes and socks. Then she tugged on the waistband of his pants and he let her slide them down and off. Finally, she pulled his shirt up and over his head. Penelope looked down at his naked body and nearly purred out loud.

God, he was beautiful. Everything he'd always been in her many, many fantasies. His body was muscled just right from shoulders to chest, to stomach to thigh. Dark hair lightly furred his chest, forming a trail that led down to a dark nest of coarse hair from which his cock sprung—standing at full attention. It was thick and long and topped with a lovely plum-shaped head that begged for kissing and licking.

She went to her hands and knees on the bed and took him into her mouth. She sucked and laved him, drawing him greedily into the recesses of her mouth. He tasted so good. Her tongue explored the wide vein that ran down its length and ran around the plum-shaped head, tasting the salty bead that pearled on the tip. She couldn't get enough of him.

His hands tightened on her shoulders and he let out a deep, rumbling, sexy groan. She suckled the base of him, drawing first one of his balls into her mouth, then the other. Her pussy throbbed with need. She whimpered.

Aidan moved so fast he was a blur and Penelope found herself flat on her back with her legs spread. "Oh yes," she breathed, closing her eyes. "Please, Aidan."

He worked his finger around her pussy, spreading the juice she'd wept for him around the entrance of her vagina. He slipped a finger in her and she tossed her head back and forth on the bed. He slid another finger into her and worked them in and out slowly, widening her. She moaned.

"More, love?" he asked thickly. " You want more?"

She dug her fingernails into his forearms. "Please."

He removed his fingers and set the head of his cock against her slick opening and pushed himself within just a little. She ground her hips, wanting friction.

He gritted his teeth and a muscle in his jaw worked. "I'm trying to be gentle," he ground out. "You're a virgin."

"Don't be gentle," she sobbed. "Just come inside me. Please."

He eased into her a little more and came to her hymen. She wiggled and sobbed at the same time, spreading her legs impossibly farther apart. "Please!"

He thrust. Hard. Impaling her nearly to the base of his cock.

She threw her head back into the pillows as her back arched. Her fingernails raked down his forearms and the scent of his fresh blood filled the air, mixing with the blood of her sacrificed virginity. She noticed that with her heightened senses. Aidan must've noticed it too because he let out a sound almost like a growl, low, deep and dangerous.

He grabbed her wrists and pinned them against the mattress. His hips remained motionless, thrust into her as deep as she was able to take him. "Are you all right?" he asked through gritted teeth.

She relaxed and moved her hips. "Perfect." It felt so good to be intimately joined with him. She'd never felt closer to another human being than she did to Aidan at this moment.

He rocked his hips back and forth and slowly let his thrusts get longer and harder in slow, steady strokes. The thick, rigid length of him plumbed the depths of her pussy unrelentingly. She moaned and gripped the blankets on either side of her, spreading her legs as far as she could. She wanted nothing more in the world than what his cock was giving her pussy.

Her first orgasm came quick and hard. She was helpless under the force of it. It racked her body, made her cry out. Her vaginal muscles clenched and released around his cock and moisture flooded her sex.

Before she knew what was happening, he'd slipped out of her and was kneeling between her spread legs. The first touch of his tongue against her heated flesh made her hips buck. He laved over her and delved his tongue into her opening. He suckled her clit, exploring it with the tip of his tongue and then sucking on it. A deep, helpless moan issued from her throat and another orgasm flirted with her.

She told him how good his tongue felt on her, how perfect his cock felt inside of her. She was shameless in the way she talked to him, wicked and wanton. She used every single word she'd learned from watching the illicit liaisons of the servants in the stables on the estate. And she loved every second of it.

He licked her inner thighs, lapping up every last bit of her virgin's blood and the slick cream her orgasm had produced. He groaned deep in his throat, a satisfied, exciting sound that made her clit throb.

"Get on your hands and knees," he told her.

She complied, spreading her knees far apart and pushing her buttocks into the air.

He caressed her rear and slipped one finger up and down both her openings, circling each in turn with deliberate slowness. Aidan drew moisture from her pussy and spread it around her anus. She shuddered with pleasure and anticipation.

"Later," he promised in a dark voice.

He slipped a finger into her pussy and hooked it around until he found some place within her that made her gasp. "Do you like it when I touch you there, Penny?" he purred confidently.

In response she merely moaned and nodded.

He caressed the spot, rubbing it back and forth and she climaxed again merely from that one little action performed only by his fingertip. While pleasurable tremors still racked her body, he slipped his shaft into her and thrust into her as far as he could go. He grabbed her hips and drove into her hard and fast over and over. By now, the entire building must know he was fucking her senseless by the noises she made.

He reached around and played with her breasts, massaging and gently pinching her hard nipples. His hard hot chest pressed against her back. Another climax was on the horizon and her breath came in little pants, her muscles tensed.

His hands brushed the hair away from her neck and he licked the sensitive skin between her shoulder and throat. As her next orgasm broke over her body like an earthquake, he bit. The pain of his teeth breaking through her skin magnified the pleasure of her climax. She gasped. An ecstasy she'd never known possible swept through her body as he drew blood from her. It crashed over and infused every cell of her body and invaded all the recesses of her mind until her reality was only pleasure.

His cock pulsed inside of her and hot sperm flooded her. He pulled her down with him onto the bed in a tangle of limbs. His mouth still sealed on the flesh of her throat. Her vision clouded and nearly blackened.

"*Mon ami, desist.*" Gabriel's voice entered her consciousness. Gabriel was not in the room. Was he speaking within her mind?

She looked up, trying to focus. She wanted to protest Gabriel's command, but somewhere deep down she knew Aidan had to stop.

"*You have more to do before you are through with her, oui? You cannot do the rest if she's suffered so much blood loss she loses consciousness. Control, mon ami. Control. Take more than she is able to give and you wilt the rose.*"

Aidan's pulled his mouth away from her, and bit his own wrist. Thick blood welled and to Penelope it smelled like the finest wine. Aidan lowered his wrist to her mouth and she licked it, letting the sweet, coppery taste of his life-force fill her mouth. She made a sound of appreciation in her throat and latched her mouth to it.

She laved and sucked at his wrist. He wrapped his other arm around her, tucking her against him protectively. The hard length of him caressed every inch of her bare body. His cock was still thrust into her pussy as far as it would go from behind.

The blood flowed into her. At the same time she felt her body dying, it morphed into something else. She was being renewed, reborn. Her old life fell away like an old winter coat she didn't need for warmer weather.

Her consciousness flickered and threatened to extinguish. Her hold on his wrist faltered and her eyelids dropped.

"Will she be all right, Gabriel?" she heard Aidan ask within her mind.

Gabriel heaved a sigh. "*Yes. You Embraced her so well, mon ami, I must go now and find a woman to fuck for the entire night. Remember. Her first feeding of the morning will be of paramount importance. Make sure that she receives it. When she awakes, it will be to Monia's line. She will be a fully Embraced part of our family.*"

Penelope let Aidan's wrist slip away and darkness took her.

* * * * *

Penelope rolled over and snuggled into something soft, hard and warm. Arms came around her and pulled her close. Lips brushed her brow and a hand smoothed the hair away from her face.

She felt so safe, protected and loved. Her eyes fluttered open, then closed again. Smooth lips brushed hers and she came more fully awake. Blue eyes met hers.

Memories flooded her—of the last week, of Aidan, of what they'd done last night. She should've been appalled at her behavior and faint with the drastic changes that had been wrought in her life, but something, her mark maybe, calmed her, helped her to accept what was happening.

All the same, she recoiled from him and sat up. Realizing she was nude, she hastily pulled the covers up to cover her breasts. Aidan leaned up on an elbow and smiled his sexy, knowing little smile at her. A dimple popped out on his cheek. "Are you all right, this morning, Penny?" he asked. "You're looking pale."

Something gnawed at her stomach and she realized with a jolt that she was hungry...and not for food. Not the normal kind, anyway. Horror coursed through her.

"I've been Embraced, haven't I?" It was more a statement than a question. She knew the answer because she was incredibly aware of the pulse in his throat and the blood that that ran through his veins.

"I'm a monster now. Like in the penny bloods. Like in the folklore. I'm a demon. One of the undead."

He sat up and the sheet slipped down to his waist, revealing his hard, muscled chest, the bones of his pelvis, and the line of fine hair that led to heaven. He crossed his bare arms over his knees, emphasizing his biceps. Penelope swallowed hard, suddenly aware of far more than just the pulse in his throat.

"Yes, and no, Penny," he said. "Forget the folklore and the penny bloods, none of that is true. You are hardly undead. Immortal, yes, after a fashion. You can still die, although you won't age. Undead, no." He shook his head. "Though it feels like we are dying when our marks are triggered, we are not undead. Your body has morphed into what it was meant to be since the day you were born. The blood you took from me last night wrought the changes. Gabriel will be able to explain things to you better than I can. You will feed, we will dress and then we will go see him."

"Feed?" Hysteria nearly overcame her. "You don't mean share a breakfast with you, do you? You don't mean eggs and a bit of dry toast, washed down with tea." She leapt from the bed and pulled the first thing she saw over her head, one of Aidan's shirts, and buttoned it. His scent, which seemed even more pronounced this morning, enveloped her and made her dizzy. He smelled so good. She grabbed the back of nearby chair, trying not to collapse.

He was there in a flash, moving much faster than a human ever could. He braced her against him, making the onslaught of his delicious scent against her nostrils even harder to take.

When he spoke, his voice rumbled through his chest and against her. "No, I don't mean eggs and toast. You are newly Embraced and weak. You need blood to sustain you, make you stronger. You must feed the *sacyr*."

She shook her head. "I won't. Do you hear me? I won't take blood from a human." Even as she said it, she could hear the blood coursing through his veins, hot, potent, and powerful. It made her mouth water.

His arms tightened around her. "Then take the blood of an Embraced. Take mine."

She sighed and shook her head. "I'm not taking blood from anyone."

Aidan took her by the shoulders and gave her a little shake. His blue eyes glowed with a power they hadn't had before. "You listen to me now, Penny. You've always been stubborn, but I'll not have that now from you. Not when your health is at stake. A week ago my life changed forever, just as yours did last night. Do you think I wanted this?" Anger made his accent more pronounced.

She shook her head.

"No. I wanted my own stables, my own horses and land. Do you I think I can ever have that now? Can you see a member of the Vampir raising horses? It bothers me, yes, but there's something bigger here, Penny. Something that puts all my petty desires to shame and you know what it is. You're going to have to accept your fate. I don't have to tell you why. I'll bet anything you saw it when your mark was triggered."

Penelope shuddered. "On the coming equinox the Dominion bleed through." She'd felt that force like a poisonous cloud scrabbling at the edge of her consciousness, wanting nothing more than entrance into her mind. Not to kill her, nothing so simple as that. It wanted to consume and suck away every last bit of joy from her existence, all her love and compassion, all her memories and experiences. If the Dominion prevailed on the equinox they would not kill, oh no, nothing so easy as that. They'd make the world no fit place to live and everyone would desire death. Everyone would kill themselves.

"Yes. The Vampir evolved long ago out of a need for humans to protect themselves from the Dominion. We are the only thing standing between humanity and Hell. You were born marked for this responsibility, Penny, as was I."

He was right, of course. No marriage lay in her future. No titled lords. No children. Gone were the beautiful gowns and the enchanting soirées. Gone were the gilded parlors and the carriages drawn by matched bays.

Her eyes narrowed. "You did this to me. I was marked, certainly. In some strange way I understand that. But my mark never had to be triggered. This never had to happen to me." Even as she said it, she regretted it. She knew well that Aidan hadn't purposefully triggered her mark.

Guilt flooded his eyes and weariness etched itself into lines of his face. "I know. I didn't mean to do it. I never had any intention of Embracing you. It just happened. It was the lust between us, the desire."

Her legs gave out and he held her up. "I...I have to sit down," she whispered.

He helped her over and sat her on the edge of the bed, then sank down beside her.

She shook her head. "The worst of it is that I realize now that I'm not a lady, not at all, Vampir or not. Thinking the thoughts I've had about you even before I came to New York, I was never a lady. I truly am the wicked person Horatia always said I was."

"You listen to me, Penny. You're not wicked."

"After what we did last night...out of wedlock...in a house of ill-repute? The worst part is that I should be mortified beyond words. If I were a lady, I should regret every single second of it. I should bow my head in shame. But I don't regret it. Not at all. I must be a horrible person, Aidan. I must be—"

Aidan covered her mouth with his, stopping the flow of her words. His lips were hot on hers and silkily smooth. He rubbed them over hers and curled a hand at the nape of her neck, bringing his mouth more fully to bear upon hers, possessing it skillfully until she let out a little moan from the back of her throat.

He pulled away and set his forehead to hers. His breath came harsh and aroused. "Having your sweet body beneath me and against me last night fulfilled every fantasy I've had in my life. All I can think about is when we can do it again. You'll always be *my* lady, Penny. Always."

She should've been offended to be called a stable hand's lady. But she wasn't. Pleasure and pride suffused her instead. That's when Penelope threw all her *should be's* and *should've been's* away. And if that made her wicked...so be it. Then she was wicked. What Horatia had taught her didn't serve her here in this strange new world. Perhaps it was time to slough off her teachings. They'd never suited her anyway.

So Penelope opened her mind and embraced the storm she'd been thrust into. She'd always liked storms, anyway. Like the child she'd once been, she realized she'd been born for something more than the drawing room, formal teas and impossible societal expectations. A peaceful feeling of surrender stole over her. She sighed. She was free at last of her old life.

The hunger that curled in her stomach had been growing steadily ever since she'd awoken. It gnawed at her and seemed to make her very veins ache with the desire to feed.

"You're pale," Aidan pointed out. "You're resisting the demands of the *sacyr*."

She shook her head. "I'm fine."

"You're not. You need *sacyr* to survive."

"What's *sacyr?*"

"Nourishment, life-force. It's what keeps the Vampir alive. We hover on a dangerous precipice, Penny. Nearer to both heaven and hell than humans. We protect humans from the Dominion, and in return humans sustain us."

She didn't understand. Her head swam. His pulse beat in his neck and she fought the urge to nuzzle his throat, bite, and drink deep. Time slowed as it had the night before. Her senses became clearer and more pronounced. Were these symptoms of blood hunger?

His fingers went to the buttons on her shirt. One by one, he popped them open. She heard the button slide through each hole, heard the movement of his skin on the material. She felt the shirt come open and the cool air hit her exposed breasts. His arms wrapped around her waist and he pulled her into his lap so she straddled him, her knees resting on the mattress. Her pussy brushed his hard cock and she wanted him inside her.

She placed her hands on his shoulders, levered up and pushed herself down on his cock. She was tender from the night before, but the pleasure of his shaft filling her overrode the pain.

He let out a quick hiss of air that ended in a groan. "You'll be the death of me, woman," he growled.

She settled in his lap with his cock thrust all the way up inside her, resting at the very base of him. Her breasts brushed his chest, and his dark hair caressed her bare nipples. He arched his neck, throwing his head back. "Do it, Penny. I know you want to. C'mon, love."

She stared at his throat and wiped her clammy palms on her thighs. She salivated and her fangs lengthened. Her eyes grew wide at the foreign sensation of those two tiny points emerging and extending. She explored one with her tongue and cut herself for her efforts. Her own blood flooded her mouth, and the scent of it filled the air.

His gaze snapped to hers. Vibrant blue eyes stared at her mouth. "Do you think I'm not also hungry?" His voice held an edge of danger. He took her mouth with his and slipped his tongue within, lapping up every bit of blood she'd drawn and sucking on her tongue until her womb contracted with desire. She moved her hips, wanting friction.

His hand found the nape of her neck and worked its way up to tangle in her unbound hair. His fingers gripped the hair at her scalp gently, and he pulled her head back, exposing the long line of her throat to him. At the same time, he worked his hips back and forth, driving his cock in and out of her as much as he was able in the position they were in.

It was enough. The head of his cock rubbed against the place of sensitivity far up within her and the flesh at the base of his cock brushed her clit. It was heaven. He licked her throat from her ear to her collarbone. "You *will* feed on me, Penny," he murmured against her skin. "I'm going to force you to."

Before she had a chance to wonder what he meant, he reared his head back and came down on the tender flesh of her throat. His fangs pierced her skin and sank in. It hurt, but the pain passed quickly into pleasure…and morphed into ecstasy. She gasped. The sensation flowed up from her pelvis and out from his mouth as he suckled gently from her throat and rocked her back and forth on his cock.

The sweet scent of her blood filled the air once more. This time it was much stronger.

That's when Penelope knew what he'd meant. It was irresistible, undeniable. She had to feed. She bent her head to the curve of his neck and felt her fangs lengthen even more. She set them to his skin and bit. His body tensed and the suction he kept at her throat let up momentarily before resuming with passion. She rose a little, bracing her weight on her knees and allowing the speed and depth of his thrusts into her swollen, wet pussy to pick up.

Blinding, white-hot pleasure filled her as surely as his blood filled her mouth. Latched and connected at both pelvis and vein, they became one being, sharing the same blood. Her orgasm burst over her like a tidal wave, bringing him with her and submerging them in mind-numbing pleasurable release. She felt his body tense against her and his cock jumped within her pussy, releasing a stream of hot ejaculate. Her pussy absorbed every drop of moisture he had to give.

Sated, they pulled their mouths away and rested against each other, breathing heavily. A glorious languid power flushed her and she felt lazy as a jungle cat that had just fed well and now lounged in the sun.

She pulled away from him and laid a kiss to his lips. He lifted her off of him and she experienced a sense of loss when his cock slipped free of her body.

"Do you feel better?" he asked.

She could do nothing but smile at him. She felt wonderful. "I feel as though I've drunk absinthe."

"This feeling of euphoria you have will last a while, but soon you will grow hungry again. It is the curse of the newly Embraced. The power of the *sacyr* is very strong at first. I am only now starting to learn how to control it and Gabriel says it is early. Most newly Embraced don't learn to control it for years."

"So why are you doing it?"

He shrugged, stood, and headed to the bathroom. "Gabriel thinks I'm different than the others."

Chapter Six

Penelope followed Aidan into Gabriel's darkly lit chamber. Heavy drapes blocked the glow of the sun and candlelight flickered over the rich silk covered furniture and the rumpled bedclothes on the enormous four-poster bed dominating the room.

Three nude women lay upon it, their limbs tangled carelessly together as they slept. Penelope glanced away, a blush coloring her cheeks.

"What? I am expected to connect mentally with you two in all your lustful glory last night and not revel in a little of it myself?" Gabriel tsked. "I think not, my little rose."

She searched the darkness for the source of the disembodied voice. Her eyesight was far better today than it had been the day before. Still she could not see him. Suddenly he seemed to float straight from the shadows toward her. She forced down the surprised gasp poised in her throat.

Aidan stepped forward. "I brought Penny so you can answer her questions."

"What questions do you have?" He turned toward the bed and regarded the slumbering Demi-Vampir. Penelope knew they were Demi, could feel the special energy that emanated—like hungry stomachs growling and demanding to be fed.

"I understand I am now Vampir—"

Gabriel turned and regarded her. "No. You don't understand. You were always Vampir. You were born Vampir. It simply lay dormant within you until the time came for your mark to be triggered and for you to be Embraced by your brethren. But make no mistake you were never fully human."

"But my parents were not Vampir," she argued. "They *were* fully human. I do not understand how this could be."

"The marks are handed down through families, like eye or hair color, but sometimes a mark might not show up in a child for hundreds of generations. In Aidan's case, he and his mother were both born with cauls. However, his mother's caul signified that she had second sight rather than identified her as a future Embraced, as it did Aidan. Indeed, the marked are very rare. Rarer still for two marked individuals to have been born so close to each other and have been so intimately linked since birth. It leads me to believe there may be some kind of confluence of events here, events related to the coming equinox."

"What about the Demi-Vampir?" she asked. "They were not marked, correct?"

"Most were not, *non*. As I was not marked. Humans who are Embraced, if they are not strong enough, will become Demi-Vampir. Just as one whose mark is triggered and not Embraced directly afterward will also become Demi-Vampir. The Demi feed off sex and lust. The fully Embraced feed directly from human life-force."

"So now my destiny is not to belong to one of New York's finest families, make my mark on the city's society and marry well. Now it is to feed from the life force of humans and also protect them from the Dominion." She didn't bother to keep the horror from her voice.

Gabriel smiled. "But, my dear, you now belong to the finest family in all of Vampirdom. Do you not realize there is no line any more highly respected than Monia's?"

Penelope looked away. That meant nothing to her. "Tell me about the Dominion."

Gabriel shrugged. "There is not much to tell because their purpose is simple. They are like us in some ways, but instead of feeding from life force, they take something far more precious. The Dominion survive by extracting the higher emotions from humans — feelings of love, contentment and happiness. They are what humans think of as Hell. In times long past, the Dominion have collapsed and extinguished entire civilizations with their ravenous feeding. The Vampir evolved from humans in order to fight the Dominion, and in exchange humans sustain the Vampir. Humans are prey in so many respects." Gabriel shook his head. "Surprising they haven't become extinct by now. But the Dominion and the Vampir need them."

"In what way?"

"Well, it is not productive to kill off one's sole source of nourishment, is it? And of course, it is from humans that marked Vampir are born."

"What of the Dominion? How are they born?" asked Penelope.

"The Dominion are ancient beings and, as far as I know, were never born. They do not reside in this reality fully, but live on the fringes, always looking for a way in. They work through dreams mostly. Except for certain, thankfully, infrequent times when the veils are thin enough for them to come through and wreak havoc on mankind. This close to the equinox they can possess weaker humans, as well. Some of the stronger ones can possess humans at will at any time."

Penelope put a hand to her aching temple. She couldn't understand why she knew some things and not others. It was the effect of her mark, she suspected, but it didn't make it any less overwhelming. "The Dominion work through nightmares most of the time, don't they? They can extract a person's very will to live, can't they?"

"*Oui*." There was pleased surprise in his voice. "I wonder if you will be unusual and strong like Aidan, Penelope. You two are most intriguing, I must say. A unique couple like you coming to us right before the equinox. Most fascinating."

"The Vampir are powerful enough to take over the human race, aren't they?" she asked with slight horror.

Gabriel nodded. "And some families have tried. They are stopped by executioners, fully Embraced like Niccolo, the man who found you. Punishment for attempting such a thing is meted out swiftly and without compassion. Niccolo is not a man to have against you."

Penelope was tired of talking of this. Tired, and frustrated. "I have a friend who lives on the streets. He helped me when I was lost. I would like to help him now."

"Charlie?" asked Aidan. He didn't sound happy.

"Can we?" Penelope asked Gabriel. "Can we bring him here, to the Sugar Jar?"

"Does he enjoy sex? The Demi would appreciate anyone they can feed from. He could live here, eat well and, in return, serve them. It would not be unpleasant for him."

She frowned. "I don't know if he would want that."

"Well, bring him here and we'll find out, all right?"

One of the women on the bed roused and made a little purring noise. "Gabriel, come back," she murmured in a sleep-roughened voice. She raised a slender hand to her breast and rubbed a hard nipple, pulling at it with long, elegant fingers.

Gabriel walked to the doorway and ushered them through it. "I have things to attend to. Go now and find your Charlie. I will deny you nothing, my sweet Penelope. I think you will be a strong one like your lover here. The plot thickens, eh?"

With those cryptic words delivered, he shut the door.

* * * * *

Penelope squinted against the bright sunlight on the street. She seemed far more sensitive to it today than she had yesterday because of her heightened senses. Everything smelled and tasted stronger. Everything sounded louder and she felt things at a finely tuned level. It followed suit that the bright sunlight reflecting off the snow affected her somewhat badly. It was not unbearable, but not comfortable, either.

She blinked, trying to focus on the people who passed them on the street and the carriages going clacketedy-clack over the cobblestones. She felt different, yet in some respects, the same. A part of her felt removed from the world around her. In the world, but not of it.

She touched her neck, feeling for the puncture wound Aidan had made, and found only smooth, unbroken skin.

"We heal quickly, Penny," said Aidan. "We can heal most wounds, unless they're very grievous. We can even heal minor wounds in each other and in humans."

"Incredible," Penelope murmured, rubbing her throat. That explained why the bruise on her face was completely gone and her head no longer ached.

Strong hands cupped her shoulders. Aidan's heat bled through the material of the fine coat she wore, given to her by Gabriel's Demi servants, clear through the fabric of her dress and straight to her skin. "I know what you're feeling right now, the disorientation and the depression. You have been reborn. Even though your mark smoothed the way for you, it is still a hard transition to make."

She swallowed hard. "Let's just find Charlie." She pulled way from him and walked down the streets, her warm, fur-lined boots crunching over the fresh snow.

Aidan pushed his hands deep into his pockets. "Are you strong enough to be doing this?"

She shrugged. "I feel stronger than I ever have. I just want to find Charlie." She set her jaw. She wouldn't let harm befall him, not after all he'd tried to do for her.

"This Charlie must mean a lot to you."

"He's a good friend."

Aidan fell silent and Penelope followed suit. She'd check the alley they'd slept in the night before the first encounter with the policeman. If he wasn't there, she'd check Winder's. After that…well, it would be time to try out the new extrasensory abilities she had as Vampir.

She watched a carriage pull up to the curb. A glimmering of something unseen physically but tangible within her mind stopped her in her tracks.

"What's wrong?" asked Aidan.

"I don't know."

A beautiful, well-heeled woman stepped from the carriage in front of *Mrs. Bishop's*, a dressmaker's shop, and surveyed the street regally. Her light blond hair had been coiffed and curled to sit perfectly beneath her fancy, feather-plumed hat. A long, luxuriously expensive winter coat sheathed a body Penelope suspected turned the heads of many men.

Without a glance in their direction, the woman entered the dress shop, causing the tiny bell attached to the top of the door to jangle. Wordlessly, Penelope went to stand in front of the glass, watching.

Behind her Aidan sighed. "Penelope, you have to let it go."

Aidan thought she was being wistful. Indeed, she had every right to be. That woman had not a care in the world beyond what color ball gown she would have made and which invitation she would accept in order to best show it off. But it was nothing so superficial that had Penelope standing at the window. It was something...*else*. Something she couldn't quite comprehend.

Her lips curled into a semblance of a bitter smile. "And why shouldn't I be wistful, Aidan? My entire future has been wiped away with nary a bit of my own consent."

Penelope watched a dark-haired woman, undoubtedly the owner, look up from the counter and smile. Penelope was aware of the inhabitants of the shop to an incredible sensual degree. She fancied she could hear the sound of that smile, her soft skin crinkling with the action. She could the rustle of their skirts, the sound of their boots on the floor...even though she stood outside looking in.

"Miss Agatha," the plump, happy woman exclaimed, walking around the counter to clasp her hand warmly. "So very nice to see you today! You know you are one of my favorite customers."

Agatha closed her eyes for a moment, almost seeming to bask in the glow of Mrs. Bishop's happiness. She sighed. "And it is always my pleasure to visit, Mrs. Bishop. You know your dresses and gowns are my most preferred. You always outdo yourself!"

Pride suffused Mrs. Bishop; Penelope could feel it even through the glass. "What can I do for you today?"

Agatha walked to the opposite wall and ran a finger over the myriad bolts of colorful fabric. "Oh, I had the whim to have a ball gown made, and perhaps a couple of afternoon dresses. The styles are changing, you know. I want to stay in fashion. I'd like some dresses with high collars and puffed sleeves." She turned with hopeful eyes to regard Mrs. Bishop — round, rosy face with bright, soulful blue eyes, cupid's mouth and a doll-like demeanor. No one refused her anything; Penelope ventured a guess. "Could you do that for me?"

"Of course. Let me take your measurements again. I need to update my files. Your figure grows more lovely every time I see you, Miss Agatha."

Agatha tittered, covering her perfect bow mouth with a gloved hand. "You flatterer. Where is your charming young daughter, by the way?"

"She's here. Caroline?" called Mrs. Bishop.

A small girl, about five, with large, dark eyes appeared around a corner. She smiled shyly at Agatha. Such love radiated from Mrs. Bishop and her daughter, such tender hearted, strong happiness...steady contentment. It warmed Penelope.

Agatha bent at the waist, resting her hands on her thighs. "Hello, Caroline. Are you being a good girl?"

"Yes, Miss Agatha." She ducked her head beneath the counter and back up as though playing peek-a-boo.

Agatha and Mrs. Bishop both laughed.

"What fabric would you prefer for your ball gown, Miss Agatha?" asked Mrs. Bishop.

Agatha turned, setting a finger to her bottom lip and bracing her other hand on her waist.

"Hmmm...I'm not sure. You have additional bolts in the back room, don't you?"

"Yes."

"Could I see them?"

"Of course."

Agatha turned and allowed Mrs. Bishop and Caroline to lead her into the dusty, dark back room.

Penelope frowned as she watched them walk away. Why didn't she feel right about this? On the surface everything seemed fine...but there was something wrong here. Something not right emanated from Agatha. Something hungry, almost like what she felt from the Demi, but darker.

"Penelope, I'm sorry for your loss. I really am. If I could take it all back, I would." Aidan's low voice rumbled through her, as his body touched hers. His warm hand fell once more upon her shoulder. The feel of it had Penelope closing her eyes.

Something evil dwelt behind blue eyes. Something crept up upon the unwary. Something shifted into a thing feared, a thing of nightmares. Fear radiated from the back room of the shop, innocence lost....

Penelope eyes popped open and she moved, knocking Aidan's hand from her shoulder.

"Penny?"

Without a word or a backward glance, she entered the shop and headed for the back. Aidan followed her.

"Can't you feel it?" she whispered.

Aidan's brow furrowed. "I feel nothing but annoyed at the moment."

She shook her head. "I feel—" She gasped as a rush of cold darkness touched her soul as it had when Aidan triggered her mark.

She headed for the back room. The shadowy darkness swallowed her. Her eyes adjusted quickly and she noticed she could see much better in the dimness than she could only a day ago. She pushed aside a red curtain and the stench of fear stuck in her nostrils and clung like frigid cobwebs to her heart. Shivering, she searched the storage room for the source of her unease.

Then she saw it. Three figures crowded into the corner of the room. Two voices whimpered pitifully.

Penelope wasted no time. She stalked straight over and wrenched Agatha away from them with a strength that shocked her. Agatha reeled back and hit a wall, letting out a very unladylike growl. In the shadows Penelope could see her lovely young face as it contorted and changed into a hideous mask. Her lips peeled back to reveal dark, crooked teeth. Her eyes grew dark and lost their humanity. Her cheeks hollowed, leaving her cheekbones in sharp relief to her face. It growled. A low voice issued from its throat. "How dare you pull me away from them."

Penelope's heartbeat jumped in her chest. She fought the urge to back away. "Get back, Dominion," she said, stepping between the thing and the two figures crumpled in the corner. "You're not going to hurt them."

It laughed. A frightening, scraping sound. "A newly Embraced Vampir. I can feel your youth, child. You're no match for me. I am as old as the mountains and the depths of the sea."

"You'll be surprised how strong I am, Dominion. I'll give you a taste of it right now," she bluffed. Her insides felt like jelly in the face of this creature. But she couldn't show her weakness.

It took a step toward her, another growl trickling from between thin, pulled back lips. It sniffed the air. "I smell your fear, child. It clings to you like a heavy mantle. You're no match for me."

Out of the corner of Penny's eye, she saw Aidan enter the room. "What do you want from these people...from me?" she asked.

The Dominion pierced her with soulless black eyes. "I'm going to take your memories, Vampir, all your joyous ones. The first time you rode Daisy. The French doll your father brought you when you were ten. I'm going to take your first kiss, and the first time you rode bareback with your hair loose." She cocked her head, blond curls falling into one eye. "I want *you*, love, can't you see? All the good parts. I want them all."

Penelope shuddered, then straightened her back and lifted her chin. She stepped forward. "Well, you can't have them."

"I take what I want." The Dominion laughed.

Aidan stepped to Penelope's side and its laugh died in its throat. "Two," it rasped.

Aidan cocked his head and smiled. "Two," he confirmed.

It scuttled along the wall, toward the door. Aidan blocked it and pressed it against some tall shelving lined with bolts of fabric. It fought him, scratching him and growling. With his massive strength, Aidan pinned it down. "Feed, Penny."

"Wh...what? Feed from that?"

"You feed from it and I'll feed from it and together we'll push the Dominion from Agatha's body. The woman's been possessed. The Dominion can't stand to be in a human body being fed on by a Vampir. It will vacate."

She stepped forward and knelt in front of the thing. It struggled and keened in Aidan's arms, but was unable to free itself. Penny took its wrist in her hand, feeling the blood pulse under the skin. Her fangs emerged and Penelope bit. Warm, dark, sweet blood coursed into her mouth. It was ecstasy.

Penelope knew when Aidan bit Agatha's throat because their minds became joined. A dark force pushed at them, trying to break through, tried to feed from them, but was unable. Penelope felt the rage of the Dominion like ice over her skin. Beneath that was Agatha's own bewildered consciousness. Letting pure instinct guide her, Penelope pushed the Dominion back using her mind. Aidan joined her and together they forced the grip the Dominion had over Agatha to dissipate. The harder Penelope and Aidan pushed, the harder the Dominion held onto Agatha.

Finally something screamed in Penelope's mind and echoed through Aidan's. Shards of light burst in her mind's eye. Penelope felt blind and deaf from it. Penelope and Aidan flew back from Agatha as though hit by the force of a carriage drawn by eight horses at full speed, and hit the floor.

Silence.

Penelope lay for a moment, regaining her vision and hearing. Tentatively, she sat up, cradling her head and groaning. Beside her, Aidan mirrored her movements.

"Did we…did we force it out?" she asked him.

Aidan looked over at Agatha and Penelope's gaze followed. The woman lay in a heap on the floor. Her face was serene and framed by her lovely golden curls. No outward sign of the Dominion remained. "I think so." He shook his head as though to clear it. "That was incredible. How did you know?"

Penelope paused. How had she'd known? She wasn't sure. "Let me think about that, Aidan."

She stood and went to Mrs. Bishop and her daughter. They, too, lay unconscious on the floor. Penelope could tell they still lived. She felt their life force ebbing strongly through them both. "Will they be all right? The Dominion took something from them. I can feel it."

Aidan stood and walked to her. "It took some of their emotion, a little love, a little joy, a few good memories. If you hadn't stopped it, they'd be a lot worse off than they are now. As it is, they'll feel the effects of the attack for a while, and will permanently lose some memory, but it will not be nearly as bad as it could've been."

"Will the Dominion target them while they sleep in order to take the rest? Through nightmares?"

Aidan shrugged. "We can't know, Penny. The power of the Dominion is great right now."

"How can we just leave them here like this?"

"We won't. Now is a good enough time as any for you to learn how to use glamour."

Aidan patiently taught Penny to use her skill of glamour, which was a bit like something called mesmerism she'd seen a demonstration of once in London. They positioned Agatha, Mrs. Bishop, and Catherine near each other. When they awoke, they would simply rise, resume their conversation, and search for fabric as though the Dominion had never been present. Although Mrs. Bishop and Catherine would both experience a marked melancholy and exhaustion for days to come.

* * * * *

Aidan pushed the door of the dress shop open for Penelope. Thoughts swarmed through his mind. If they'd run into the Dominion so easily, just walking down a random street, then the Dominion must be everywhere right now.

"You never explained how you knew the Dominion had entered Agatha," he said.

Penelope frowned and turned toward him. "I could feel all three of them, sense their emotions. I felt there was something wrong with Agatha. She was empty, hungry, in a way that seemed strange for a human. She...coveted. Agatha was like an emotional pit of despair. She needed to try and fill herself up at any cost. Mrs. Bishop and her daughter gave off a feeling of true contentment that Agatha seemed drawn to." She cocked her head at him. "Isn't that what you felt?"

Aidan frowned. "I don't have this ability. I've never heard of an Embraced who can sense the emotions of humans or sense Dominion."

"Well, I can, apparently. At least, I can sense humans. I don't know about Vampir." She gazed at him speculatively. "Feel something."

Aidan grinned. Little did she know what he felt any time he was with her. "All right, I am." As though he could simply start, or stop, for that matter.

She closed her eyes and Aidan's gaze traced the sweep of her ginger-colored lashes across the blush of her cheek, and trailed to her full, shapely lips. How good that mouth had felt, kissing his lips, his skin…his shaft. Aidan stifled a groan.

Penelope's eyes popped open. "No, nothing. I don't feel a thing."

Aidan closed the distance between them and cupped her cheek in his palm. "Then you're the only one."

She took a step back, out of his reach, and shook her head. "Not here. Not in public. Don't forget yourself, Aidan."

He took her by the hand and led her into an alley running alongside the shop and pushed her into a shadowed doorway. "This better?" he purred.

She pressed her body against his, and he had to stop himself from yanking off her many layers of winter clothing. He wanted to be inside her now. He wanted to thrust into her slow, so slow she could feel every little ridge of his cock brushing against the walls of her pussy. He wanted to do that until she went insane and cried out his name, until she came hard all over him again, and again, and again.

He put that on his list of things to do in the very near future.

Gently, he pinned her arms against the wall on either side. He leaned down and brushed his lips against hers and breathed in the sweet scent of her breath. When the Embraced took blood their bodies changed the life force into an intoxicating scent. "I'm going to take you slowly next time. I want to torment and tease you until you're begging me to take you hard and fast," he murmured. "I want to move so slow you practically lose your mind."

She shuddered against him in pleasure and closed her eyes.

"What am I feeling now?" he teased, pressing the hard length of his erect cock against her pelvis. "Can you tell?"

She laughed. "Not through all these clothes, I can't."

"Let's go take them off, then."

She looked up at him and the expression gracing her beautiful blue-green eyes spoke of passion, bewilderment...uncertainty. "Oh, Aidan," she whispered. "What are you doing to me?"

"Right now, a lot less than I want to be doing."

Penelope turned her head and looked past him. Aidan followed her gaze. At the mouth of the alleyway a well-heeled couple had paused to stare at them. The woman held a glove-clad hand to her mouth in shock. The man harrumphed and led the lady on, clearly in awe that such unsavory characters should have wandered into his part of town.

Aidan looked back at Penelope and caught the pained look in her eyes right before she averted them. He released her and drew a hand back through his hair. What *was* he doing to her? He wasn't good enough for her. Not even when they'd both been Embraced and were not a part of the human world any longer. No, still, he wasn't near good enough for the likes of Miss Penelope Coddington. Silly to think they could find happiness together. She needed someone far better than the likes of him.

"Aidan, what's the matter?" she asked.

Aidan shifted. His clothes fell to a heap in the middle of the alley and he flew up in the shape of a crow. *"Come on, Penny,"* he said telepathically. *"Let's find your friend. I'll look from the sky if you look from the ground."*

Chapter Seven

With Aidan working from the sky and Penelope working from her enhanced Embraced senses, at dusk they finally found Charlie leaning against the back doorway of a restaurant. Snow had been falling steadily and now coated Charlie's slumped form.

Penelope gave a cry of joy and ran to him. Aidan, still in crow form, lighted on a nearby lamppost and watched.

Penelope touched Charlie's shoulder and a sharp crystalline thread of sensation thrummed through her. She drew her hand back, her brow furrowing. "Charlie?" she asked. "Charlie? Can you hear me?"

Charlie's eyelids fluttered open and he smiled. His face was beaten severely. Obviously, the policemen hadn't done much of anything except rough him up further. Or possibly some other bit of misfortune had befallen him since Niccolo had rescued her.

Charlie reached up and touched her cheek. "Beautiful Penelope, you've come back for me?" His words were slurred. Perhaps he was delirious?

"*He's dead stone drunk,*" answered Aidan. Even in her mind his tone was smug, self-satisfied. "*Your friend is soused. Can't you smell it?*"

Penelope sniffed. Aidan was right. "Can you stand, Charlie? I want to take you to a place where you'll be safe."

Charlie reached up and rubbed his thumb across her cheek. "I still think you're the prettiest thing I ever saw," he slurred. "I've thought of nothing but you since you left. I even spent the coins I had on liquor instead of food to try and forget your pretty face. I was so afraid you were dead."

"I'm not dead, Charlie. I'm here and want to help you. I want to bring you to see some friends of mine. Can you stand?" she repeated.

Charlie struggled to his feet and leaned on Penelope. His hood fell back, revealing his face in all its beautiful grotesque glory.

"Are you all right?" asked Aidan. *"Can you get him to the Sugar Jar alone?"*

"It isn't far. I should be able to get him there. You can't shift back right now, anyway. It would be a bit draughty for you without any clothing."

"Who is he? His speech sounds educated, cultured. What's he doing out here?"

"He was cast out from his family because of his facial deformity. He's a Scythchilde."

"Hmmm…another glorious one. I'm sure you two have much in common." Aidan flew toward the Sugar Jar, not allowing her to respond.

Charlie got himself to the Sugar Jar on his own, for the most part. Penelope had to aid him only occasionally. The good thing about the Tenderloin District was that no one really paid her and the stumbling drunk beside her much attention. In the Tenderloin, such sights were commonplace.

Penelope handed Charlie into Gabriel's care, who appointed several Demi-Vampir to attend him. Gabriel assured her they would not feed from him until Charlie was ready, if he ever became ready.

Penelope made her way back up to Aidan's room to strip off her soaked clothing. The melted snow saturated even the dress she wore beneath her cloak. Aidan had disappeared as soon as the Sugar Jar had come into sight. Penelope had felt his hunger. It was far more acute than hers. Perhaps he'd gone to feed?

She slipped her wet coat off and hung it over a chair near the fire to dry. Snowflakes drifted past the window outside, but within the room it was warm, snug, almost domestic. Penelope picked up one of Aidan's shirts that he'd hung carelessly over a chair and pressed it to her face, inhaling his scent—soap and spice, the scent that was uniquely Aidan. It never failed to comfort her.

She wanted it against her skin. Setting the shirt aside, she slipped out of her ankle-high boots, stockings, corset, undergarments and dress. Then she picked all the pins out of her hair and set them on the table by the fire and shook her long, wet hair out to dry.

Penelope slipped Aidan's shirt on and buttoned it. The sleeves hung way past her fingertips and the

bottom hit her mid-thigh. It felt erotic to be wearing his clothing. She hugged herself, rubbing the material against her upper arms and sighing.

Hunger rippled through her and she mentally tamped it down. Despite her hunger, she still could not bring herself to feed on an unsuspecting human.

She simply couldn't do it.

A pecking sounded at the glass of the window and Penelope whirled. A lone crow stood on the sill. She crossed the floor to the window, and opened it.

Aidan flew in. She closed the window and turned. Her eyes bulged and her mouth went dry. Aidan had shifted and stood in the center of the room in all his naked glory. Would she ever not be in awe at seeing him nude? He was absolutely magnificent. She couldn't help but peruse his body from his toes to his head. Her gaze caught on his strongly muscled thighs, his tight stomach and sculpted arms and chest. But the thing that intrigued her most was his cock, thick and long, now stirring and becoming hard under the heat of her gaze.

He crossed the room toward her silently and stealthily, his gaze holding hers. When he reached her, he placed a finger under her chin and closed her mouth. "You're wearing my shirt," he murmured, running the back of his hand down her cheek.

Penelope blushed and tried to back away from him. He held onto her upper arms and kept her in place. "I...I...needed to change out of my wet clothes, so I put on the first thing I could find," she lied. She didn't want to admit she'd put his shirt on simply to be closer to him, have the scent of his skin close to hers.

Aidan released her. "Did Gabriel settle your friend in?"

"Yes."

"He's marked, you know."

"I did feel something when I first touched him, a sort of tremor went through my body."

Aidan nodded. "Yes, I could feel it even without touching him. Right now, so many of the people around the Tenderloin are marked. It's the equinox, drawing them all near. Most of them make their way to Gabriel and the Sugar Jar, either by their own will or someone else's."

"Like I did," said Penelope.

"You didn't feed yet did you?"

"I'm not hungry," she lied.

"Penelope, I fed before I came back here so I could help you feed unburdened by my own needs, and that's exactly what I intend to do. You can't feed from me again so soon. We need a variety of blood types to satisfy the *sacyr*."

She shook her head. "Really, I swear I'm not hungry."

"I don't believe you."

She cocked her hip and rested a hand on it. "Before I was Embraced, did I eat as much as you?"

"Probably not."

"Then as Vampir, why would you think my feeding habits would mimic yours?"

He went silent and frowned, obviously not liking that she'd made a legitimate point. The fact that it wasn't true she'd ignore for the time being. She needed to work herself into the idea of feeding on a human. She just needed a little time to adjust.

"Well, are you sleepy, then?" he asked.

After such a long day of fighting the Dominion and looking for Charlie, she couldn't deny it. "Of course I am. I'm exhausted."

She found herself swept into his arms in the space of a heartbeat. "Then let's go to bed. I don't want you to get weak," he said.

He settled her in the bed and, still naked, he curled himself around her. Penelope lay in a state of contentment like she'd never known before. Soon Aidan's breathing deepened and steadied. A smile played around her lips as she matched her breathing pattern to his. Could one fall in love so quickly? Was it possible? On that thought, sleep took her, enveloping her like a strong, dark cloud.

* * * * *

Penelope awoke with a gasp, perspiration coating her face and neck. She sat up, inhaling the fire-warmed air of the bedroom and taking in fast, hard gulps of air. Grief closed over her and sucked her down, consuming her completely. She wanted to cry, but couldn't. She could do nothing but breath, in…out…in…out…. She concentrated on it and tried not to think about the weight that had settled in her chest.

Aidan sat up and rubbed a hand over his face. "What's the matter?"

Penelope couldn't answer him. She focused on her breathing and tried not to let the heaviness of what she felt overwhelm her.

Aidan sat forward and his voice lowered. "Penelope, what's wrong?"

"Can the Dominion attack the Embraced?" she whispered hoarsely.

Aidan went silent for several heartbeats before answering. "Yes, if they're weak. If they haven't fed when the *sacyr* has called to them. Yes, then they are vulnerable."

Penelope closed her eyes and tried to force the sob up from where it had lodged in her throat. If she could cry maybe the pressure would be released.

Aidan pushed a hand through his mussed hair, mussing it further. "They would target you, Penny. If they know you can sense them the way you did in the shop today, they've realized you're dangerous to them. They won't let you go unpunished."

She nodded once, quickly losing interest in the subject, and laid down on the bed, curling herself into a ball. What did it matter anyway? She just wanted to lay here and sleep….

Aidan shook her shoulder. "No, Penny. You can't go back to sleep. You must feed."

She mumbled at him. She didn't have the will to feed. She didn't have the energy for anything but to lie here and drift off.

Aidan swore under his breath and left the bed.

When Penelope became aware once more it was because Aidan was shaking her again. "Penny, please sit up."

But she felt so heavy….

Strong hands lifted her. She flopped against Aidan's chest and felt the grief bubble up again, threatening to overwhelm her. Her eyelids fluttered open and Aidan's concerned face blurred and came into focus.

Another pair of strong hands braced her shoulders and Penelope forced herself to look at their owners. Niccolo's face came into her view. Vaguely, she wondered where his cat was.

"She's sleeping, *mia cara*," he answered the question she'd asked in her mind. He looked at Aidan and shook his head. "They've really got her, Aidan. She's far gone. Everything you've gone through today is no good for a newly Embraced, even for ones as strong as you two. It has drained her, made her weak."

"I found Niccolo and asked him to come here to feed you," said Aidan. "His blood is old and powerful. It may give you strength enough to beat back the Dominion who have sunk their claws into you, Penny. You must feed on him. Do you understand me?"

What was he talking about? Why couldn't he just leave her alone? Her eyes fluttered shut.

Aidan passed her onto Niccolo's lap. Niccolo bent his head and pressed his throat to her mouth. "Feed."

She noted dispassionately the five o'clock shadow on his face and the scent of man. His blood pulsed beneath his skin, thick and sweet. But she truly did not feel hunger now. Now, all she wanted was oblivion. She let her eyes close and her head fall back.

Niccolo reached behind him, took something from the table by the bed, and scratched it across the flesh of his throat. Blood welled, filling the air with strong scent. It reached down through all the layers of her grief, grabbed onto her hunger and shook it like a dog with a bone.

She roused and watched as it beaded on his skin, gathered weight, and dripped down, but she couldn't gather enough strength to partake of it. Niccolo smeared his finger through it and rubbed it over her lips. "Come on, *mia cara*. Eat."

She licked her lips clean and Niccolo drew her head to his throat. Penelope lapped at the blood with the tip of her tongue, sending a shudder through Niccolo's body. The taste of it filled her mouth.

Centuries of feeding gave Niccolo's blood a special flavor, rich and dark.

She latched onto the slight wound he'd made and sucked. Her fangs extended and she sank them into his neck. A sound of muffled satisfaction came from her filled throat, mixing with a groan of pleasure from Niccolo. Penelope knew well the ecstasy of being bitten. She wondered if Niccolo felt it now.

"Yes, it's heaven," answered Niccolo. "*Dio*, heaven."

The words made his throat work, and his Adam's apple bob. Penelope bit harder, drawing another groan of pleasure from Niccolo's throat. She clawed at his chest like a kitten at her mother's nipple, trying to get as close to Niccolo as she possibly could.

"That's a girl, Penny," came Aidan's concerned voice behind her. "Drink deep and grow strong. I'll not lose any part of you to those bastards."

The blood did seem to push the grief away. The dark storm clouds lifted from her mind, causing the immense sorrow to dissipate. With the release came the threat of racking sobs. The fact that she'd have to stop feeding to allow them was what kept them at bay. Instead, she focused on the sweet life force coursing into her body from Niccolo's—the blood mixture of thousands of humans. She felt Niccolo's age run through her. He was an ancient one, powerful to a degree neither she nor Aidan could imagine. Through his blood she felt the effects of all those years, the joy, pain, sorrow, anger, love, and lust.

It was this last that she found mirrored within her own bloodstream—a powerful lust for Aidan that she'd yet to satisfy. She wanted him. She wanted his naked body against hers, his strong hands tracing over her breasts, exploring her pussy. A shudder of pleasure went through her that had nothing to do with the ecstasy she felt at taking blood. She grew hot and damp between her legs at the thought of Aidan fucking her. Her breasts became heavy and her nipples tightened. A whimper rose up in her throat.

Niccolo pulled her back, so he lay on the bed against the pillows, and Penelope straddled him on all fours. Aidan's shirt slid up with her movement and now revealed the tender flesh of her pussy to Aidan.

"She is burning for you, Aidan," said Niccolo telepathically.

Aidan's hand slid over her buttocks and glided down to caress her sex. He slipped one finger within her and she moaned.

"God, Penny," Aidan cursed under his breathe. "I want to taste you." He slid his finger out of her, over her folds and up to bathe her clit with the moisture. Back and forth he stroked it and Penelope felt the blood surge into it, making it grow larger and more sensitive.

Niccolo groaned. He braced his hands on her waist and rubbed his body against hers. "How much torture am I expected to take? I can smell your desire, Penelope."

Penelope whimpered and let loose of Niccolo's throat with a gasp. The magic Aidan was working over her clit was intensifying, building, until the last vestiges of the Dominion were gone and pure, animalistic lust had replaced it.

Niccolo brushed a kiss across her forehead and gently turned her over to lie between his spread legs. "Give her relief, Aidan," he said.

Aidan knelt on the bed, still clothed in the pants he must've hurriedly donned before leaving the room. The sight of his bared chest and forearms as he crawled toward her across the bed set her heart racing. He slid a hand over one of her thighs. "Spread your legs for me, love," he commanded darkly.

She complied, letting the air bathe her sex. She felt Niccolo's pants rough against her legs and buttocks, and the hard bulge between his legs where his cock had hardened. The flesh of Niccolo's bare chest warmed her back through the shirt she wore. Niccolo's fingers went to the buttons of her shirt and undid them, revealing her aching breasts with their tight, rose-tipped peaks.

Aidan made a growling sound deep in his throat as he lowered himself between her thighs. The first lick he bestowed made her arch her back and gasp.

Niccolo cupped her breasts and massaged, drawing the tips out and rolling them between his fingers. As he manipulated her breasts, he murmured things softly in Italian near her ear. Aidan licked along her pussy, lapping up all the moisture she'd made for him. His tongue played along the opening of her vagina, slipping in from time to time, and flicking over her clit, teasing her.

The combination of sensations, Niccolo's hands on her breasts, kneading and teasing, and Aidan's dark head between her thighs, his skillful tongue pushing her toward climax, made Penny a mass of pure uncontrollable want. She moaned in ecstasy.

Aidan slid a finger within her and then another. Very, very slowly, he thrust in and out. His mouth settled over her clit. He licked, and then sucked it, flirting with it with the very tip of his tongue.

Penelope came apart. She bucked and moaned under the force of her climax. Aidan rode her through it, lengthening it with his fingers and tongue until she was nearly blind with the intensity and length of her orgasm.

She came down slowly and lay there, relaxed and panting. Aidan left her, but a dark, predatory look graced his dark blue eyes. Penelope knew well he wasn't finished with her yet.

Niccolo brushed another kiss across the crown of her head and slid from beneath her. He stood, his pants bulging conspicuously.

Penelope pulled herself up to recline on the pillows, still warmed from Niccolo's body, and pulled Aidan's shirt closed. Her lips twisted into a smile that was a half grimace. "I've turned into a proper whore, haven't I?" However, none of the horror she should've felt came with the truth of those words.

"Mia cara." Niccolo shook his head. "Still human ideas of right and wrong cling to you. This was merely the result of being newly Embraced coupled with the coming equinox. Not even I, an ancient Vampir, can control such energies right now." Niccolo bowed his head. "I apologize for impinging upon your bond. I confess I wanted to play with your body more than I did, but I held myself back with much effort. I don't want to break the sacredness of what you two share."

Penny lifted her head. "Bond? Sacredness?"

Niccolo walked to the door. "I will leave you now. You should be safe from the Dominion with my blood coursing through your veins, giving you strength. However, I must insist you do not deny the *sacyr*. She is a hard taskmaster and will lay you low if you resist her."

Penelope looked away. "I understand that now."

"Good. Lesson learned." Niccolo left the room and shut the door behind him.

Penelope's gaze swung to Aidan, who watched her like a cat would watch a cornered mouse. He did all but lick his lips. "For this night, you are mine," he promised with hooded, intense eyes.

Penelope opened her mouth to say, *for every night*, but he had dropped his pants and the sight of his silken steel cock once again stole her breath. On his hands and knees, he crossed the bed toward her.

"For—" she started. Aidan slipped a hand to the small of her back and slid her down off the pillows, flat beneath him, with one strong pull. Penelope gasped. "For every night," she finally pushed out.

"*Tonight,*" he repeated a fraction of a second before his mouth came down on hers. His tongue plunged between her lips and sparred with her tongue possessively. He parted her legs and settled himself between her thighs. The head of his cock sat at the hot entrance to her core.

"I've never wanted a woman as much as I want you, Penny," Aidan murmured into her ear. "Do you want me too?"

Penelope moved her hips, rubbing herself against his cock. She wanted him inside her. "Don't tease, Aidan," she implored. "You know I want you."

He pushed the very head of his cock into her and slid one hand down between their bodies to play with her clit. Using her juice, he massaged the nub until it was huge and swollen once more.

Penelope whimpered and moved her hips. Her hands found his buttocks and she tried to push him inside her. Aidan braced himself up using his knees, keeping the head of his cock just slightly pushed within her, and snagged her wrists. He pinned them above her head and held them there with one large hand, letting the other trail down to leisurely explore her breasts, outlining every hill and valley of the distended nipples with the tip of his index finger. At the same time he rocked his hips, moving his cock in and out of her minimally.

He was teasing her beyond all reason and it was maddening. "Oh, God, Aidan," she cried. "Don't make me beg."

"Ah, but you see. You have no say in the matter, do you?" He squeezed her wrists lightly. "I've got the upper hand in this. I can do anything I want. I can play with your beautiful body for as long as I wish."

His hand strayed down and circled her anus. Penelope's heart skipped a beat. She'd never considered that area to be a place of pleasure, but, oh, the sensation rippling through her now was nothing but...just as it had been the first time he'd touched her there. He slid a finger within carefully and thrust. At the same time, he moved the head of his cock in and out of her. Her eyes fluttered shut and she moaned in helpless pleasure.

"Do you like that, angel?" he asked.

Penelope nodded. "I like anything you do to me."

"Hmmm...good," he purred. "Because there's so much I want to do to you."

"Then *do* it," she implored.

His only answer was to lightly squeeze her wrists, reminding her who was in charge.

She moved her hips, trying to force his cock deeper within her. When her efforts proved fruitless, she used the only weapon she had at her disposal.

She licked her lips in calculation before she spoke. "Aidan, I need to feel your cock inside me," she said in a low, silken voice. "I want to feel you thrusting in and out of me, making me moan your name. I want you to feel me when I come, how my muscles contract around you, how wet I get. I want—"

Aidan's eyes darkened and he thrust hard into her, impaling her to the very base of him.

Penelope closed her eyes and hummed her approval. "Oh, yes, Aidan. That's it." She opened her eyes to a smile playing around his beautiful lips. "Witch," he accused.

Slowly, mind-breakingly slow, he worked his shaft in and out. She fancied she could feel every ridge, every vein of his gorgeous cock as it brushed the walls of her pussy. She wiggled her still confined wrists. "I want to touch you."

He released her and she trailed her hands down his chest, playing with his nipples and running over his smooth muscles. In awe, she explored every inch of him, thinking how lucky she was to have a man like him care for her.

She looked up into his eyes and saw the truth of that caring. They held each other's gaze as he moved within her. Every once in a while, he'd shift his hips, causing the tip of his cock to rub over a different area. With her eyes and breath she guided him until he hit the spot deep within where it felt the best. He worked that spot, running over and over it with his cock. It was the most intimate erotic experience Penelope could imagine.

Her climax built slowly, like a volcano getting ready to explode. She held his gaze until it burst and she threw her head back into the pillows, closed her eyes, and moaned out her orgasm. Aidan's groans met hers as his cock jumped within her and he let loose with his own climax.

"Oh, Aidan," was all she could say.

He came down beside her, their legs still tangled and his cock still imbedded within her. They lay together, panting and enjoying the aftermath. She reached up and smoothed his hair away from his forehead as he idly stroked her breast.

"Are you all right, Penny?" he asked.

"Mmmmm...very."

"Are you still afraid? Can you sleep?"

Penelope stiffened. The images the Dominion had sent her in her nightmares crashed through her mind. Aidan lying with his throat slashed, Daisy lying broken at the bottom of a cliff. "I don't know."

Aidan disentangled himself from her and she shivered. He pulled the blanket up over her. "You're not all right, are you?"

She shivered again, but this time it had nothing to do with the cold. She felt like a child who'd woken from a nightmare and didn't want to go back to sleep. She shook her head.

"Should I have a bath drawn for you, then?" He smiled and a dimple appeared in one cheek. A hank of dark brown hair fell over his eye. "I'll wash you, if you'd like, then cuddle you up in a towel and bring you to bed with me. It'd be my pleasure."

Nothing in the world sounded better to her than that. Not evenings among the glittering court of New York complete with champagne glasses and cultured conversation. Not fifteen new gowns of the finest silk and lace. Not a handsome, titled lord offering marriage. No. To be bathed and cuddled by Aidan O'Shea was the pinnacle of her dreams.

Penelope smiled. Yes, she might just love this man. Her smile faded as dazed realization hit her. No…she *did* love this man. She'd *always* loved him.

A pained and terrified male shout sounded from somewhere down the hallway. Penelope bolted from the bed and grabbed her wrap. "Charlie," she breathed. "That's Charlie's voice." She yanked the door open and bolted down the hall, pulling on her wrap as she went. Aidan followed close behind, after pulling on a pair of trousers.

Penelope rounded an open doorway and took in the situation. Charlie lay in the center of the room on the floor. His face was turned to the side, the handsome half exposed. Monia stood over him, her throat stained with blood. Energy radiated from Charlie's prone body. He'd been Embraced. Penelope could tell by the way he felt.

"Is he all right?" she asked Monia. "I heard him yell."

Monia looked at her. Her face was pale and drawn. "It was not an easy time for him. I haven't had one resist like that in a long, long while. But he's all right. I wanted to wait until he was stronger, but he hallucinated that I was you and his lust triggered his mark."

"His lust? You mean his lust for me?"

"Yes. He was unrestrained because of the liquor and allowed himself to feel things he would have ordinarily repressed. It was that combined with being surrounded by so many of his Embraced brethren. Once his mark was triggered, I had to Embrace him."

"Of course, Monia. It's not your fault," said Aidan.

Charlie groaned and shifted. Penelope walked to him and knelt. She reached out and smoothed a piece of hair away from his sweat-dampened forehead. He moaned and tossed his head, revealing the other side of his face. Penelope gasped.

Aidan came to stand beside her. "What is it?"

"His…his deformity is…gone. It's like he never had one."

"I wondered if that might not happen," said Monia. "Like illness, at times scars and deformities are removed when a marked is Embraced."

"Amazing," breathed Penelope.

"I will leave you now." Monia put a hand to her wounded throat. It looked deep and painful. "Charlie should sleep for a while, and I need to get cleaned up and rest a little myself."

"Sleep well, Monia," said Aidan. "We'll take care of Charlie."

Aidan scooped Charlie up into his arms as though he weighed nothing. He settled him onto the bed and backed away to stand beside Penelope.

"He looks so beautiful without the deformity," she said. "He looks how his father wanted him to look. If he'd been born without it and accepted into his family, he'd be the catch of all New York society."

"He's handsome man, sure. Handsome, well born, and well bred. A gentleman through and through." Bitterness traced Aidan's tone and emotion made his accent more pronounced.

She turned her head to regard him. His hands were clenched at his sides. "Are you all right, Aidan?"

He visibly relaxed his jaw and hands. "Fine, Penny. Just tired."

"You can go to sleep. I'll stay with him." She looked back at Charlie. "It's probably better he sees a familiar face when awakens anyway."

Aidan went silent for several long moments. When he finally spoke, his voice was soft and tight. "Fine, yes. That's how it should be. You stay with him, Penny." Aidan turned on his heel without another word and left the room. She stared at the empty doorway. Was Aidan jealous?

"Penelope," moaned Charlie.

Her attention snapped back to the man still in the room. Charlie tossed his head back and forth. She laid her hand to his chest. "Wake up, Charlie."

"Penelope!" Charlie yelled, his eyes coming open. Penelope jumped up and back in surprise.

Charlie grimaced and put a hand to his head. "Penelope? Is that you? What happened?" Realization clouded his features as he remembered. "Oh."

Penelope sat on the edge of the bed. "Much has changed, Charlie. Give it time. I'm still trying to sort it all out, too."

Charlie looked up at her and grinned. He was so perfectly handsome, any woman's dream. Although, not hers. "Funny enough, I feel good. I feel like something had been missing from my life and now I've found it. I always felt different and thought it was because of my deformity. Now I think perhaps it wasn't that at all. I feel like I've…."

"Come home?"

"Exactly."

Penelope rose, located a handheld mirror, and gave it to Charlie. "As I said," she said softly. "Much has changed."

He didn't say a word as he raised the mirror, looked into it, and lowered it back onto the bed.

* * * * *

Aidan slammed his fist into the wall and broke the plaster. He left it there and leaned up against the wall, bracing his forehead against it. The violent action made him feel better, released a small portion of the anger and frustration he felt.

He couldn't have her.

Even now, after he'd had her body repeatedly, Aidan knew he'd never really *have* her. He'd never have her heart completely.

He simply wasn't good enough, because deep down, nothing had truly changed. He was still the stable hand and she was still the pampered child of wealthy England, a member of the class that looked down on filth like him. She deserved better. She deserved a man with the proper blood running through his veins, a man with the right name.

A man like Charles Scythchilde.

Aidan pulled his fist out of the wall, turned and leaned against it. Too bad he loved her so damn much. It would make letting her go, watching her fall into another man's arms so much easier if he didn't.

Chapter Eight

He'd been gone for five days. Penelope pushed aside the sheer curtains of the sitting room window and searched the street for Aidan's familiar form. She wished she knew what had happened to make him leave the Sugar Jar. She'd probed for him with her mind, as had Gabriel, but he was shut down, blocked. He wanted no one to contact him.

When she'd gone back to his rooms after finding Charlie and had discovered Aidan's clothes missing, a heavy weight had settled in her chest that hadn't lifted. What had she done to drive him away? Every night since he'd left, she'd curled up in his bed, searching the pillows and blankets for his scent.

"Penelope, are you all right?" Charlie asked from across the room.

She turned to look at him. He was pale. He would probably require a feeding again soon. In Charlie, she'd watched what it was for a normal Embraced. He was weak, like a newborn kitten, vulnerable to the world and constantly needing to feed. She hadn't allowed him to take blood from her. It was too intimate an act...too sexual. She couldn't think of Charlie that way.

She smiled. "I'm fine."

"You're looking for that other one...Aidan, right?" His voice held a note of jealousy she didn't like.

She turned away and examined a small porcelain cat on an end table. "He's a friend of mine."

"Yes, you told me," said Charlie wryly. "A *friend*."

She shrugged. "A friend." She turned back to him, trying to chase the sadness she felt from her eyes.

"Why would a friend go off this way without telling you, Penelope? Leaving you to worry the way you are. You look gaunt. Your face is pale and drawn."

She shook her head. "I don't know, Charlie. I don't want to talk about it, all right?" She forced some lightness into her voice. "Gabriel told me you want to visit your parents this afternoon? That they're here in town?" She walked over and sat beside him.

He nodded. "They're staying at the house they keep here. I want to show my mother my face." His eyes darkened and his voice lowered. "I want to show my *father* my face."

"How will you explain the change?"

His well-formed lips twisted into a rueful smile. "I don't know, an act of God? I don't care. I just want to see my father's expression when I come face-to-face with him. I want him to know I survived."

"I think you should go. I think it will be good for you, sort of cleansing. A consummation of your old life and the beginning of your new one."

His hand covered hers. "Will you come with me?"

She stiffened at the touch of his hand on hers. She bolted from the chair and went to the window. "Of course I'll come with you." She pushed aside the curtains and searched the streets for any sign of Aidan.

Behind her, Charlie stood. "Then let's go before I lose my nerve. I can't stand to see you like this, anyway. A change of scenery might distract your mind a little." He sounded angry, resentful.

She let the curtain fall back into place. "You have no claim over me, Charlie," she said without looking at him.

"I never said I did," he said lightly. It was a complete change in tone.

Penelope turned to see him smiling at her, all the tension had left his voice and body posture. Maybe she'd imagined it all? "Let's go."

* * * * *

They used the Sugar Jar's hansom, driven by one of the Demi servants. They pulled up to the grand townhouse that Charlie said was his parent's New York City residence. He'd insisted they dress well, and they had. Gabriel's funds seemed limitless and he'd dressed them like the members of high society they'd been until recently. Penelope smoothed the fine midnight blue fabric of her dress over her tightly corseted waist. A matching fashionable hat sat on her coiffed tresses, and a heavy, expensive winter cloak sheathed her. Thoughtfully, she fingered the edge of the fine garment. If she let her mind drift, it was as if the last few weeks had never happened. She could well imagine Charlie as a suitor. That he'd picked her up from her great-aunts home to bring her here to his parent's residence for tea.

The imaginings did not hold the allure she thought they would. Instead, she found her mind drifting back to Aidan and how she felt when he held her in his arms. Love had stripped away the shallow falsities of her life, left her to see where true happiness lay. Anger flared within her. Damn Aidan for leaving!

"Penelope?" Charlie placed his hand to her forearm.

She blinked. The Demi had opened the door and now held a hand to her. Wintry air filled the cab, but not even that had pulled her from her thoughts. She took the Demi's hand and stepped out of the cab, pulling the collar of her cloak around her throat with a gloved hand.

They stood on the sidewalk, looking up at the stately townhouse. Charlie cast a look at her that seemed to speak of both his hopes and fears.

She squeezed his hand in reassurance. "You'll be fine."

He smiled and nodded. "As long as you're at my side." Together they walked up the stairs to the door and used the brass knocker.

A tall, gaunt man answered and gasped. "Mr. Charles," he said in a hushed tone. "Your face," he exclaimed before recovering himself.

"Hello, Emory," Charlie said as though he'd never been kicked out of his family, never been cast from his home, had never lived on the streets and scavenged for food. "Are my parents here this afternoon?" he asked with haughty grace.

Emory hesitated and set his jaw. Penelope thought for a moment he'd deny them entry, but then he opened the door wider and ushered them into the foyer. "I'll tell them they have visitors."

"Tell them it's their son only, Emory. No more."

Emory paused thoughtfully, then nodded and left the foyer.

"They'll think it's my younger brother, Christian," Charlie murmured.

"I see," answered Penelope.

"Emory always did like me. He was quite angry when I was tossed out."

Penelope examined the marble and gilt bedecked foyer. It was rich...very, very rich. It was also cold. The Sugar Jar possessed so much more warmth than this place, she mused.

Emory returned and smiled. "I'll probably lose my job for this. But I wouldn't miss it for the world. They'll see you in the drawing room, sir."

"Thank you, Emory."

Charlie looped her arm through his and led her to a door on their left. He hesitated before he pushed it open, drawing a steadying breath. "Here we go," he whispered.

They walked into the lushly decorated, wood paneled room. An older, very beautiful woman sat on a blue damask settee. Penelope immediately recognized the resemblance between Charlie and his mother. The woman gasped and put a bejeweled hand to her chest.

A tall, heavy-set man with graying hair turned from the small bar in the corner of the room. His jaw dropped and his eyes widened. The glass he held slipped from his fingers and crashed to the fine wood floor. "Dear God," he wheezed.

"Hello, Father…Mother." Charlie inclined his head.

* * * * *

Penelope and Charlie left an hour later. She watched from the carriage window at the humans passing on the street, and reviewed the recent events. She still shook from the emotion that had coursed through the room. She'd felt the shock, outrage, and guilt of Charlie's father and the deep sorrow emanating from his mother.

It was the guilt that had finally broken his father.

Charlie had done something she'd never expected. He'd blackmailed his father into giving him money. Charlie had said he'd go to the press with his story, and that he could prove he was a Scythchilde. Charlie said he'd tell everyone he'd been kicked out into the street at a young age because of his deformity. How would that reflect upon the Scythchilde name and reputation?

Penelope didn't know if Charlie would've been able to pull it off, but that didn't matter. It was the guilt, not the fear of bad press that had finally forced his father to give Charlie possession of the New York City townhouse, the staff to keep it, and a sizable yearly income. His parents would vacate in a week's time and Charlie would have possession of it then. The deed would be in his name and would be in the drawing room safe, along with the first installment of his income.

Charlie was now wealthy. Very, *very* wealthy.

He'd introduced her as a woman he was courting, and had explained away his rich clothing as the patronage of a well-heeled friend. The last bit was not untrue. When they'd stammered around the question of what had happened to his face, asking it indirectly and not looking Charlie in the eye, Charlie had told them it had been the experimental work of a magnificent surgeon in the employ of his patron. Wasn't it incredible? Hadn't the surgeon done an amazing job? He'd told the lie so smoothly Penelope almost believed him.

The carriage came to a halt outside the Sugar Jar and the Demi helped them out. Charlie seemed to carry himself taller now, seemed to have more confidence.

She turned to him when they'd cleared the threshold and were peeling off their cloaks. "Doesn't it bother you to take money from them like this? It's given from a place of guilt, not love."

He shrugged, his eyes darkening with the rage Penelope knew he held locked away deep within. "He owes it to me, Penelope. I'll take anything of his, under any circumstance."

She frowned and turned from him to look at herself in the mirror, and began unpinning her hat. Charlie stood behind her and rested his hands on her shoulders. "I also did it for you, Penelope...for us."

Her hands stilled as she withdrew a pin. "What do you mean?"

"I wasn't lying when I told my parents I was courting you." He licked his lips. "I *am* trying to court you in my own, clumsy way." He bent his head to her throat and laid a series of kisses there. Penelope lowered her arms and went very still, not knowing how to handle his unwelcome advances without injuring his fragile ego or their friendship.

Another form appeared reflected in the mirror. A pair of dark blue eyes narrowed in thinly disguised anger stared at her. "Aidan," she breathed in surprise. "You're back."

Charlie raised his head from her neck and stared at Aidan's reflection. "Hello, Aidan," he said, his mouth breaking into a smile. "So nice of you to join us again." He laid a slow, deliberate kiss to the exposed skin of her shoulder while holding Aidan's gaze.

Penelope twisted away from Charlie, throwing him a furious look. "Go feed on a Demi, Charlie. You're hungry. I can feel it."

Charlie's smile faded. He didn't leave until she flashed him another look of anger.

She smoothed her hands over the skirt of her dress in an effort to disguise her unease. Aidan's shoulders were squared, his jaw locked, his hands loosely fisted. His body language screamed volatility.

"Where did you go?" she asked softly.

"I needed to get away from here for a few days is all," he answered. His gaze flicked over her. "Expensive dress, Penny. You look like your old self, though you haven't gained much weight back yet. Are you feeding as often as you need to?"

The concern in his voice softened her. "I'm fine, Aidan. I've been worried about you, that's all."

Aidan turned and walked away from her.

Penelope stared after him, stunned. Why was he being so cold toward her? Well, she wasn't going to chase after him that was for certain. She turned back to the mirror and continued unpinning her hat with shaking hands and a lump in her throat. But she wasn't finished with him, yet. He wouldn't push her away that easily.

* * * * *

Aidan made his way through the throng in the hallway of the Sugar Jar. That bit of cold flippancy had cost him. It was necessary, though. Penelope needed to let him go.

He needed to let her go.

In the days he'd been away, the place had filled to bursting with Embraced and Demi he'd never seen before. Young and old, they milled the hallways, slept in corners, and exuded their nonhumaness everywhere.

"Aidan," Gabriel greeted him. He leaned against the doorjamb of his office. "Welcome back, *mon ami*. I worried you were gone forever."

Aidan shook his head. "The equinox calls me too strongly. I couldn't stay away."

Gabriel made a sweeping gesture with one hand. "Ah, as it has called all of them."

"So I see."

"The equinox is in three days time," Gabriel said with a pensive expression on his face.

"Are we ready?"

Gabriel frowned. "No. No, we are not ready. I still don't know where the doorway will be. I still don't fully understand the role of the One. I still don't know who the One is. It could be you...it could be Penelope. You are both candidates."

"When will you be sure?"

"I await instruction. It will probably come in the form of a dream. At least, that is what the Keeper of the Embraced territory where the last Dominion bleed through occurred has told me. That one was 300 years ago, before I was even born."

"You've never done this before?"

Gabriel shook his head, shaking his long black hair around his shoulders. "No." He shrugged. "*Oui*, I've fought the Dominion when they've possessed a human, and I've beat them back in the world of dreams, but I've never fought in a battle like what is to come."

Aidan's brow furrowed. "How is it you're in charge of this one then?"

Gabriel smiled. "Do you think me unqualified?" He clapped Aidan on the shoulder. "I am Keeper of this territory. Therefore, it is my job to deal with the bleed through. Now, what about that little rose downstairs? Why did you leave her without a word?"

Aidan wanted to ask about other things related to the equinox, but Gabriel stopped the very air in his throat with his questions. He drew a breath. "Because I love her," he admitted.

Gabriel raised a brow. "I'm not following."

"I love her too much to force her into a life with someone so beneath her."

Gabriel rolled his eyes and sighed. "The newly Embraced. They never cease to amaze me with their ideas. Did you hear about Charlie?"

"No."

"He has regained his fortune. He is a very rich Vampir now." Gabriel smiled. "Not nearly as rich as I, but he's very well off."

Aidan backed away from Gabriel and started down the hallway. "You see. Penelope deserves him, not me."

Aidan turned and walked down the hallway with anger clawing at his heart. Everyone got out of his way after glimpsing the look in his eyes. He rounded the corner and went into the room he'd shared with Penelope and began packing his things.

It wasn't long before Penny's soft step sounded on the threshold. He paused as he stuffed a shirt into his bag and inhaled the sweet hyacinth scent of her.

"Aidan?"

He glanced up. "I'm clearing out the last of my things. These are your rooms now. I'll find somewhere else to sleep."

"Why?" Penelope walked to him and placed her hand to his upper arm. "Why are you leaving? I want you here."

He turned away from her, busying himself by cinching the top of the bag. He needed to cut off her attachment to him if this was going to work. It was for her own good. "Well, I can't be here," he answered. "Get Charlie to move in."

"Charlie? But, I want you, Aidan. You. No one else. Don't you know that by now?"

He turned to her. Her blue-green eyes were large and darkened with emotion. The sight of it twisted him inside. "You don't know what's good for you, Penny," he bit off.

She walked toward him. Wariness uncoiled within him as he watched her approach. He wanted to back away, but couldn't force himself to do it. Conflict tore at him. He wanted her...he wanted her so badly, but hadn't he been told over and over since he'd been a child that he wasn't good enough for her?

It was true.

She spread her hands flat on his chest. Her warmth bled through the material of his shirt, straight into his flesh. He tried to move away, but his feet were planted firmly on the floor as he absorbed her tantalizing touch. His heart rate sped up as she unbuttoned his shirt, exposing his chest. She made a small noise of appreciation deep in her throat and drew closer to him, as though trying to absorb the heat he gave off. His body tightened as arousal unfurled.

He growled low in his throat. "You're playing with fire."

She shrugged. "Fine. I can burn for you and melt your ice." She smiled seductively. "I like fire. Especially yours." She licked across his bare chest, found his nipple, laved it over and bit gently.

He grabbed her by the shoulders. "Don't."

Uncertainty flashed in her eyes "Aidan, I love you. I want you. I don't understand why you're acting this way, but I won't let you push me away. Make love to me now, please."

Aidan, I love you. I want you. Those were the words he'd always wanted to hear from her, and he couldn't accept them. That didn't change the fact that he wanted her beyond all reason.

Pressing a hand to the small of her back, he pulled her against him and crushed her mouth to his. He parted her lips immediately and plunged in to taste her sweetness. This was no tender kiss he gave her; it was a taking. A surprised sound rose from her throat and she stiffened. He tangled his tongue with hers as though trying to consume her. With a little sigh, she melted against him and kissed him back with ferocity.

His hands roved her body. The layers and layers of clothing she wore frustrated him. He wanted to feel her skin against his. *Just one more time....* He'd told himself he wouldn't touch her again, but he'd lied. She was like opium to him, irresistible to an addict.

She ran her hands over his shoulders and back, pulling at his shirt, trying to get it off. Strong want flashed through him, mixed with impatience to have her clothes off. He pushed her back onto the bed.

"You want me, you got me, love," he rasped.

He stalked to the open door, slammed it closed, and turned back to her. Her lips were swollen from their kiss and the delicate skin around her mouth was reddened from the stubble on his face. Her eyes were heavy lidded and her breath came in short little pants as she watched him cross the room toward her.

When he reached her, he cupped her chin in his hand and stared into her eyes, saying a silent goodbye. There would be no tenderness in this coupling. He needed to show her he was a coarse man. He needed show her he was too much for her to handle. That she needed a gentleman, not a working class Irishman like him. He flipped her to her stomach, grasped the top of her dress and pulled. The tiny buttons popped and flew, rolling across the hardwood floor. The sound of the expensive fabric ripping filled the room. Penelope inhaled sharply and her body tensed.

He made quick work of getting her clothing off until finally she lay on her back, warm, soft, and vulnerably nude beneath him. He rubbed and pulled at her nipples and she moaned.

"You like that? You want more?" he asked in a rough voice.

"Yes."

Her hands roved over him as impatient as he was, pushing his shirt off his shoulders and unbuttoning his trousers. Every time her fingers brushed his skin, tremors went through him. All he could think of was sheathing his rigid cock in the depths of her tight, hot pussy. The muscles of her sex would grip him so exquisitely. *Christ!* Her hands were driving him insane, pushing him over the edge. He needed to retain control.

He shot up from the bed and grabbed the long sash binding the drapes. When he returned, he flipped her to her stomach once more and caught her wrists.

"What are you doing?" she asked.

"Making it so you can't touch me and drive me crazy," he bit off. He wound the sash around her wrists and tied the other end to one of the spokes in the headboard. He rose up and looked down at her laying there completely at his mercy. His gaze wandered over her silky sweet back and heart shaped rear.

"Aidan?" she asked apprehensively. There was a note of fear in her voice that ran counter to his goal. He wanted to show her he was too coarse for her. I didn't wish to terrify her.

He caressed her buttocks and practically purred at the feel of her skin. He moved up, massaging her back, calming her. He kissed her earlobe. "Still trust me, Penny? You know I would never hurt you, right?"

"Yes."

"I don't want to untie you." He would release her if she asked, but he hoped she wouldn't. Her body relaxed. In defeat? In arousal? Aidan wasn't sure.

* * * * *

Penny lay with her head on the pillow, watching Aidan warily. Intense lust had tightened her body into a taut bowstring. All he had to do was touch her the right way and she'd come. There was a dark edge to him that she didn't like, despite her body's excitement. His face was a complex show of emotion--anger, desire, and love all warred for time in the depths of his dark brown eyes. She clung to the last of those.

He urged her up onto her knees and spread her legs. She was completely exposed to him in this position, her buttocks elevated, her head down, and her bound hands straight out in front of her. That knowledge served only to excite her further.

His finger slipped down her weeping sex. Approval rumbled through his chest as he found the evidence of her lust for him. He rubbed at her, tracing over her vaginal lips and caressing her sensitive clit.

Then, without warning, he plunged two fingers into her pussy from behind her, drawing a cry of surprise from her. He thrust fast and hard into her. She couldn't help the fluid that flowed from her body or the animalistic sounds that came from her throat. He kept one hand on the back of her neck, and her legs spread wide as he finger-fucked her from behind.

She came hard with a shout. Her hot liquid coursed over his hand.

"That's what I wanted, love," he purred. "Good girl. You'll always come for me won't you?"

Her breath came harsh. "Yes," she answered. "Always."

"You still trust me, Penny?" he growled.

"Yes," she said breathlessly. Her pussy throbbed with wanting him despite the anger in his voice. "I still trust you."

"I'm going to fuck you so hard you can't see straight. Tell me to stop now if you want me to. Soon, it will be too late."

"No. I don't want you to stop."

"You're not going to want me anymore when I'm through with you, Penny," he vowed.

She shook her head. "Not possible."

He merely grunted in response and moved from the bed. She heard his boots hit the floor and the sound of his clothing falling in a heap.

He came up behind her, covering her body with his. His hot chest pressed against her back, and his hard cock brushed her sex. "Are you ready for me, love?" he murmured into her ear.

Her pussy pulsed at his words. Yes, she was more than ready for him. Her body would never deny his. "Why don't you want me to touch you, Aidan? What's wrong?" she asked.

"You are you and I am me, that's what's wrong," he answered.

He slipped his large hands over her breasts and pulled at her nipples. Moisture flooded her pussy anew. He smoothed his palms over her stomach, around her waist and over her ass to her sex from behind. "Did you make some more cream for me, love?" He dipped his finger into her vagina. "I see you did."

She nodded and bit her lip. All she could think of was his cock sliding into her, pumping her until she came again. He slicked her moisture up with his fingers and smoothed it around her anus. "I'm going to take you here. I promised I would, remember?"

He slipped a finger into her back entrance and she let out a shuddering sigh. "Yes," she moaned.

"You really do want me to take you here, don't you?" Wonder replaced some of the darkness in his voice.

"Yes," she replied helplessly.

"You're a bad, bad girl, Penelope Coddington. Do you know that?" he whispered close to her ear. He inserted another finger to join the first and Penelope felt herself stretching to accommodate him. It was a pleasure mixed with a small pain that made her body hum with desire.

He slipped his other hand around the front of her and slid two fingers into her vagina. He thrust very, very slowly in and out of both her nether hole and pussy. Penelope shuddered in pleasure and her knees nearly gave out. She grabbed onto the spokes of the headboard as sensation bombarded her body, stealing both equilibrium and thought.

He brushed his finger against her swollen clit. "You're ready for me. Nice and open. Ready to come again," he said in a thick voice. He positioned his cock at the entrance of her pussy and pushed in. He thrust in and out slowly as he took her from behind. "I'm going to take you here first, and then...*there*," he promised.

Anticipation coursed through her, mixed with the slightest bit of apprehension. "I told you before," she said in a shaking voice. "I like anything you do to me. Anything. I just want you inside of me, part of me."

He growled and picked up the pace of his thrusts. He reached his hand around and rubbed her clit with two thick, callused fingers. The head of his cock brushed the spot inside her where it felt so good, over and over relentlessly. She came fast and hard, the muscles of her pussy pulsing around his cock. She sucked a breath in and let it out on a moan.

He pulled out of her abruptly and left the bed. She nearly wept at the emptiness of her body. When he came back he set an object to her anus. It felt large, smooth, and slightly soft.

"This is an object the female Demi use to pleasure each other. It's almost as wide and thick as my shaft and will stretch your muscles enough to take me." His voice was tight with arousal. He had to be skirting the outer edge of his control by now.

He'd slicked the object with some kind of lotion. Penelope assumed it eased the penetration. Inch by careful inch, he slowly worked it into her. It stretched her impossibly wide. He made gentle thrusting motions with it, at the same time playing with her clit. She cried out in pleasure.

Aidan groaned. "Dear god, Penny. Seeing you like this has my cock so damn hard I think it's going to break. *Enough.* I can't take any more." He slipped the object out of her and she felt the silken head of his cock at her back entrance. She thrust her hips up as far as she could in welcome.

"You're incorrigible, Miss Penelope Coddington," he murmured in her ear. "What can I do to convince you I'm not the man for you?"

She shook her head. "Nothing."

He'd slicked the same substance over himself to make his cock slide in easier. She felt herself opening to accommodate him as he pushed himself further and further within. When he was finally sheathed within her fully, he let out a low growl. He started to thrust. She whimpered at the complex sensation of it—the pleasure and the pain.

He stilled. "Are you all right?"

She nodded. She didn't want him to stop.

He resumed thrusting, and groaned deep in his throat. His hands tightened at her waist. "God, Penny, every single bit of you is so sweet and hot."

She pushed back against him, wanting him further inside her, wanting him to thrust harder, faster. Her clit was sensitive once again and on the edge of climax. She would never have believed her body was capable of accepting so much pleasure all at once.

"Please," she said. She didn't know what she was pleading for.

He reached forward and untied her hands. She braced herself on the bed, wishing she could touch him, but in this position that was impossible. All she could do was hold on under the onslaught of the bliss he now gave her body.

He could touch her, however. He slid his hand around her front, played with her breasts, and then went further down, sliding over her weeping, hungry pussy and delved his fingers within. His thrusts into her anus picked up pace as he fucked her pussy with his fingers at the same time and rubbed his thumb over her clit.

The sensations combined were almost too much to bear, too much an assault on her senses. Penelope's body exploded in ecstasy. She nearly screamed when she climaxed. He came with her, yelling out her name. She felt his cock pulse within her and his hot stream fill her.

He stayed within her for only a moment afterward. Their breathing sounded harsh in the suddenly still, quiet air of the room. He brushed his lips against the nape of her neck once, and then pulled free of her body.

She turned to watch him pull on his trousers and pick up his bag.

"Aidan?" she asked.

He didn't answer. Cold swept through her previously hot body. She pulled a blanket over her nakedness, suddenly wishing to hide her vulnerability from him.

"Aidan?" she asked again, her voice breaking with emotion.

He stalked to the door and opened it, his boots and his bag in one hand. He paused in the doorway, glanced at her, and then was gone.

Again.

Penelope clutched the blanket to her. He'd drawn blood, but it was straight from her heart this time, not her throat.

Chapter Nine

Gabriel walked through the battle like a ghost.

A circle of heat parted the sea of blood. Hatred ripped the edges and passion pulsed in the center. The One spiced the air, changed the cold to hot, and chased away the Dominion with their love and their lust. He caught a flash of Vaclav, cleaving the air with his claymore, saw Monia fighting at his side, blood streaked across her lovely cheeks and mouth, her eyes wild and filled with battle. He saw the Demi fighting, killing, and dying. He saw Niccolo take the Dominion out one-by-one with cold methodical precision, employing the near charmed blade he used for battle.

Heat continued to rise from the center of the circle, weakening the Demi, forcing them back. The One wove their spell, shared the power of a Vampir Love Bond.

Would it be enough? Was The One strong enough to defeat them?

A tall, gaunt Dominion with an open mouth as dark and hungry as time itself came at him with claws outstretched. They pierced Gabriel's shoulders and The Dominion's mouth came down on his chest and bit, sucking...sucking....

Gabriel came awake with a start and sat up, breathing heavily. Sweat coated his face and chest. Sarah, one of the Demi he often took to his bed, roused and rubbed his back with her palm.

"Gabriel, I hunger," she murmured. "Aid me."

Gabriel threw the edge of the blanket back and stood. "Later, Sarah. You sleep now. I just had the dream I've been waiting for." Bright early-morning light streamed in around the dark, heavy curtains covering his bedroom windows. The Vampir tended to sleep until the afternoon, after the worst of the sunlight to which they were so sensitive had passed. Penelope and Aidan would likely still be sleeping, but he needed to talk to them.

Gabriel looked for his pants, at the same time searching for Penelope and Aidan's consciousness within the Sugar Jar. When he'd located them, he compelled them from their sleep and summoned them to the parlor downstairs.

He had news.

He pulled his pants on and left the room without his shirt or shoes. He reached the parlor and several moments later, both Aidan and Penelope entered the room, neither looking at the other.

"What's going on, Gabriel?" Aidan asked.

"I just had a dream."

Penelope perched on the settee beside him. She was dressed in her nightgown and wrap. "So did I, Gabriel, but I didn't feel the need to wake the house to tell someone about it."

"Not that kind of dream, my rose." Gabriel smiled and glanced at them both. "You are the One."

"Who is the One?" asked Aidan. "Penelope?"

"You are *both* the One. Rather you're halves now. Together you make the One."

Aidan sat down in a chair. He was also barefoot and shirtless. He pushed a hand through his already mussed hair. "I'm not following what you're saying."

"I'm saying you two are a bonded pair. Every Vampir has a mate. We mate for eternity if we can find him or her." He smiled. "A little like wolves. Monia and Vaclav are a bonded pair. I had a mate once, but—" He broke the sentence off unfinished. He still had problems speaking of her, even centuries after her death.

"But—" started Penelope.

Gabriel held up a hand to silence her. "Let me finish. You are the One when you are bound by blood and bodily fluid. When you are connected at pelvis and vein. When that happens the world will shake and the Dominion will bow to you. You must do this on the eve of the equinox near the Dominion's doorway...amid the battle."

"This is insane!" said Aidan.

Gabriel shot him a chilling look. "There is one more thing. Her blood must be spilled on the battleground when she comes. Blood and bodily fluid, love and lust, that's the recipe for this bit of glamour—the glamour that will push the Dominion back and seal the doorway."

Aidan stood and paced the floor. "Let me see if I've got this straight. To close the doorway, Penelope and I must make love to each other in the middle of a murderous battle near an inter-dimensional doorway. Not to mention in front of who knows how many people in the dead of winter." He paused for dramatic effect and turned toward him. "*This* will save the world from the Dominion?"

"Yes."

"Aidan is right. That's insane!" declared Penelope.

Gabriel smiled and shrugged. "Welcome to the world of Vampir."

"Why us? Why can't another bonded pair perform the act? Why can't Vaclav and Monia do it?" asked Penelope.

Gabriel shrugged. "They are not the One. They are destined to fight the Dominion on the equinox. You are the two chosen for this task, no others."

Aidan rounded on Gabriel. "Why do we have to have sex to perform this task?"

"What do you think is stronger than fear? What do you think is the *only* thing stronger than fear?"

Aidan's brow furrowed.

Gabriel rolled his eyes. "Love, Aidan. *Love*. It sounds trite, but it's true. The only thing that can overcome fear is love. Love is demonstrated physically when you make love. It is a symbol, a very powerful one. There is natural magic in the act, created by thoughts and emotions blending, converging. We need you to be one with her—two halves of a whole. We need for you two to exchange bodily fluids at that spot. We need her blood split upon the ground —"

"You said that before. Her blood. Why not mine?"

Gabriel smiled. "Feeling protective, Aidan?"

"Hell, yes."

"She is the more powerful one. I hope that doesn't bruise your pride too badly, but that is why. Born with a red caul and being female makes her a very powerful Vampir. She has not realized all her strength yet. With time she will be stronger than me, stronger than Monia. That is why she can sense the Dominion and can feel the emotions of humans. That is why the Dominion targeted her, no doubt. She is very threatening to them. We need her blood to mark that battleground, willingly sacrificed in a moment of shared love."

"You're wrong," said Penelope quietly. Her voice rose, "Gabriel, you're wrong! We don't share love! He doesn't want me, let alone love me. He wanted to fuck me, that's all. Fuck the rich girl who slighted him when he was young. He made his point. He fucked me, made me want him, then he left me."

Penelope turned on Aidan and narrowed her eyes, "I don't love you either, you know. I know that now. We share nothing more than lust. And there is absolutely no way we share this bond you're talking about, Gabriel. Do you understand? No possible way." She stood and stalked out of the room.

Aidan turned and looked at Gabriel.

Gabriel shrugged. He had no part to play in this. "This is your mess, *mon ami*, not mine. I wish you joy of it. Just make sure she's pliant and wanting you by the equinox."

* * * * *

Aidan paced his room like a caged lion, replaying the image of Penelope's eyes as she'd told him she didn't love him. *Christ*, this was hard. He wanted nothing more than to leave the Sugar Jar and travel west, nothing more than to be away from the hatred and anger he'd seen in her eyes yesterday morning. But he couldn't leave. Not now. Not with the equinox tomorrow night. Every day the Sugar Jar had received more arrivals, more Vampir and Demi coming to fight. The Sugar Jar was brimming with the non-human now. Whenever a human passed the threshold, noses quivered with the scent of prey, senses tingled with the possibility of food.

He went for the door, unwilling to stay cooped up any longer. He headed for the parlor, rounded the doorway, and was instantly sorry he'd left his room. Penelope sat at the table by the fireplace, reddish-gold head bent studiously over a chessboard, intimately close to a dark, male one. She and her new suitor concentrated on the board, puzzling over what move to make next.

Aidan paused at the doorway, seeing Niccolo, Monia, and a blond haired stranger sitting together at the far side of the room.

Penelope glanced at him, and then turned back to the board as though she couldn't care less that he was there. She covered Charlie's hand with her own.

Aidan's eyes narrowed and every muscle in his body tensed. A part of him wanted to stalk over and pull them apart, sling Penny over his shoulder and drag her up to his room. Fuck her hard and fast so she knew she was his...and only his. He wanted to mark her body well. Scent her like an animal would, so no other man would be fool enough to approach her ever again without risking bodily harm.

He grimaced. *But this is what he'd wanted.* Charlie was the better man for her. Kind, intelligent, handsome, civilized, cultured, of good Bostonian stock and name. Hell, he was even moneyed now--far more moneyed than Aidan could ever hope to be.

He choked back the possession he wanted to claim over her and forced himself to look away.

Bright feminine laughter tinkled through the room. "Aidan, come here," called Monia. "I want you to meet someone."

Grateful for the invitation and opportunity to leave Penelope's immediate vicinity, Aidan walked to Niccolo, Monia, and their companion. The stranger, a tall, well-muscled man, stood.

"This is Vaclav, Aidan. Aidan, Vaclav," Monia introduced.

Vaclav held out a hand and Aidan shook it, feeling the impossible weight of Vaclav's age. This was a very old one, older than Monia and Niccolo both.

"Nice to meet you," Vaclav said smoothly. "Gabriel has told me about you, and" --his blue eyes flicked to Penelope—"the English lady. He has told me about your role to play in tomorrow night's festivities." His accent was a complex mix of flavors, impossible to hear which country he'd hailed from originally.

Aidan's smile faltered. "We will do our best to defeat the Dominion."

"Ah, *si*," said Niccolo. "That is most important."

Monia pulled a chair out and patted it. "Come, sit. Gabriel is in seclusion, trying to divine the location of the doorway. Of all of us, he is the most gifted in traveling into the Dominion's dimension to gather information. We are enjoying a drink, and speaking of what we will do on the morrow. We would enjoy your thoughts, *bel homme*."

From the corner of his eye, Aidan saw Penelope rise and walk from the room. Every fiber of his body was aware of her, every corner of his consciousness filled with the knowledge of her. Charlie rested his head in his hands and sighed. Was he frustrated with the way the chess game was going? Was he upset because Penelope was not returning his affections?

Aidan watched the edge of her pale blue gown disappear around the corner of the doorway. He should let her go, leave her alone. He should let her hate him and fall into Charlie's arms. He should sit down with Monia, Vaclav, and Niccolo and have a drink, some conversation. He should forget about Penny.

"Excuse me, Monia. I have to see to something," he said.

Monia inclined her head and smiled knowingly. "But, of course."

Aidan nodded at Niccolo and Vaclav, and then walked out of the room. Charlie's dark, sharp eyes followed him.

Passing through the Demi and Vampir that roamed the foyer and hallways of the Sugar Jar, Aidan followed the gentle swish of her skirts, remembering how easily the expensive fabric of the gown she'd worn the other day had rent under his fingers. That led to memories of untying her corset...and then the rest of what he'd done to her. Aidan's muscles tensed and his cock rose.

Would the woman continually make him hard with only the thought of her?

She disappeared into one of the pantries off the kitchen. What was she doing? He followed her silently into the small, dark room and came up behind her. He pressed her face-first against the wall and she gasped in surprise.

"What are you doing in here?" he asked against her ear.

"Can't...can't a woman get a little time alone?" Her voice was thick, as though close to tears, and angry. "This house is so crowded right now."

Aidan inhaled her hyacinth scent and closed his eyes. His hands strayed to her waist and traveled up, cupping her corseted breasts. Her breath caught and rolled out in a sigh at his touch. He could smell her desire rising, the aphrodisiac of the juices between her legs heating up the air around him.

For a few moments the only sound was their breathing, harsh in the quiet pantry. Images of all the ways he could take her in here amid the sacks of flour and sugar filled his mind's eye. How he could flip her skirts up, rip through her undergarments, and ease himself deep into her heat.

"What are you doing?" Penelope whispered. "You hate me, but you touch me like you want me." Her voice broke. "I lied the other day. I do love you. Are you happy? What more do you want from me?"

Aidan tightened his arms around her and closed his eyes. He battled with himself for a moment, wanting to tell her he loved her back. But that would damn her to life with him. Damn her to a world beneath the one she'd grown up in...beneath her, period.

"I want you wanting me tomorrow night, Penny," he murmured. Her silken hair brushed his lips as he spoke. "I want you ready to accept my body within yours. Will you be prepared for that?" He kissed her earlobe, drawing his tongue along its soft edge. His fingers massaged her breasts through her dress and corset, drawing circles around her nipples.

She shuddered against him in what he knew was pleasure. "We might not share love, you and I," she said. "But we do share lust. We can fake our way through tomorrow night. I'll be ready for you."

She turned to face him and he set both hands on either side of her head, palms against the wall. Only a sliver of air separated their bodies. When she inhaled, her breasts brushed his rib cage. "After that will you leave me alone? Let me heal myself of you?" she asked.

He studied her in the half-light. Her eyes were dark and filled with vulnerability. Her soft, lush mouth begged for his lips and tongue. Dear lord, how would he ever be able to leave her alone? How could he pull this off, this pretense of aloof uncaring?

Her hair had come loose from its chignon. He twined a finger around a red-gold tendril and pulled her head toward his. "After tomorrow night, Penny, I'll leave you alone, but not before." He captured her lips with his, rubbing over them slowly, so slowly, until she whimpered. He crushed his mouth to hers and kissed her hard, parting her lips and slipping his tongue within with a hint of the possession he wanted to stake.

Her arms came up and her fingers curled in the hair at his nape as she pressed her mouth to his. His body tightened and he toyed with the idea of stripping her without delay.

A drop of something hot and wet hit his cheek and he realized she was crying. He pushed away from her. Sorrow filled him. "This is in your own best interest. You'll be over me soon enough." Was he trying to convince her or himself?

"What are you talking about?" She put a hand flat to her cheek, maybe in an effort to conceal her tears. "What is in my own best interest, Aidan?"

"Just be ready for me tomorrow night, Penny." He turned and walked away.

Chapter Ten

Midnight coated the sky, and stars scattered the blackness like diamond chips. Aidan stepped into the street and regarded the Demi and fully Embraced that stood outside the Sugar Jar. Gabriel had summoned only a small entourage to accompany him to the site where the doorway would open. The rest of Sugar Jar's current inhabitants would follow in waves.

Aidan's gaze sought and found Penelope in the small group, standing near Charlie. She was wrapped in a long coat and her breath showed white against the frigid air.

Monia stood beside Vaclav near Gabriel, and Niccolo stood to the left of him. A handful of other trusted Demi and fully Embraced scattered the area. Some Aidan had met, others not.

Aidan edged his way around the small group to get as close to Penelope as possible without seeming too obvious.

Gabriel looked at Aidan and nodded. "Very well. We're all assembled. Tonight is a night of great importance. I don't need to drive that point home to you anymore than I already have. In the 247 years I have been Vampir, I have never seen it's like. As the Keeper of this Vampiric territory, the one in which

New York City falls and also the place where the Dominion's doorway will open, it is up to me take care of this problem." Gabriel closed his eyes and for the first time Aidan saw the grief and weight of this responsibility etched into the features of Gabriel's face. "This has fallen by default into my hands, and I will bear accountability should it fail."

"We will not fail," said Vaclav. "I have faced the Dominion before and prevailed, as have many others that will battle tonight. We are happy to do it again. We will not fail, my friend."

Gabriel opened his eyes and they settled first on Penelope and then on Aidan. "We'd better not."

Aidan met his gaze and held it. "We won't fail you, Gabriel."

"Good." Gabriel held a hand out to Penelope. "Come here, my rose. We need you to be our barometer. You will lead us to the doorway."

Penelope looked uncertain. Aidan stepped toward her, wanting to support her, but Charlie reached her before he did.

"Come on, Penny. Close your eyes," Charlie said, taking her by the hand.

Penelope closed her eyes and everyone waited. They shifted back and forth in the cold night. Snow crunched under their feet. Finally, Penny opened her eyes and spoke. She turned to the left and pointed. "That way. I feel them coming from that direction."

They moved through the streets like ghosts, directed by Penelope. They passed the homeless and downtrodden of first the Tenderloin District and then Five Points. The humans seemed to shrink from them instinctively, fading into dark alleys to escape their view and slamming and locking their doors.

Down the narrow streets and around corners they progressed. Slowly Penelope gained confidence, seemingly slipping into a near trace as she reached out with her mind and felt for the Dominion, tracking them over the city until finally she led them to the harbor. The cobblestone square she stopped in was surround by old buildings.

"Here," she said in a breathless murmur loud enough only for a few to hear. "They'll come through here. They feel very strong."

It was a business district spotted through with warehouses. This time of night, it was devoid of humans. That was fortunate.

"Niccolo, please summon the others," said Gabriel.

Niccolo closed his eyes, communicating telepathically.

Aidan walked to Charlie who stood a short distance from Penelope. "You shouldn't be here. You're too young and weak," said Aidan.

Charlie glowered at him. "I can't stay away from this fight. Especially not if Penelope is here."

Aidan's hands fisted. "Fine. Stay near her, then."

Charlie shot him a piercing look and went to stand beside her. Aidan stayed back and away, but not far enough he couldn't protect if he had to. The Dominion would harm Penelope over his dead body.

"This is the place where the veil will be the thinnest," announced Gabriel to those assembled. "It is here the door will open between our world and theirs and they will come through. It is here where we will fight them."

"What will happen if we cannot defeat them?" asked someone from the back of the crowd.

"If we allow them to leave this place and seek the company of humans, all is lost. Unchecked, the Dominion will feed with voracity and Earth will become a hell-place, full of only nightmares, misery and death. The Dominion are, indeed, what humans perceive as the spawn of hell itself."

"If they're the spawn of hell, are we the angels, then?" asked another.

Gabriel smiled coldly. "We are warriors, pure and simple. Or, if you prefer, we are the wolves fending off bears from the flock we feed upon. We protect, but only because we want the sheep for ourselves. We can pretend no benevolence here. This is about survival."

"They're here," announced Penelope. "Lots of them." Her face had gone white.

* * * * *

A pinprick of light appeared in the air, growing brighter and brighter. It began to expand, turning all the light around it black, and then consuming it. Penelope gripped Charlie's forearm as she watched it open like a hungry mouth, growing wider and higher.

"What will come out of that?" breathed Penelope.

"We won't have to wait long to find out," answered Charlie. "Look."

Hazy shapes within the doorway coalesced and solidified, faded and returned. The first of them stepped through and Penelope caught a glimpse of the Dominion made physical before it was pulled into the throng of Embraced, its life quickly extinguished. Tall and gaunt, he'd been a wisp of a creature that looked human. Dead, soulless eyes stared from an emaciated face that wore a hungry expression.

One by one they came and were defeated. Then the pace of their arrival sped up and more poured out than could be killed. The demons flowed like water from the mouth of the doorway.

Chaos erupted around her. Penelope gripped her knife and held it out in front of her, daring one of the creatures to come toward her. They all looked different, like bad, ghoulish copies of humans. One approached Charlie and raised a sword-like weapon.

"Charlie!" yelled Penelope.

Charlie turned and blocked the creature's weapon on its downward arc. As the battling couple neared her, Penelope stuck her blade into the thing's back. It fell to the ground like a rag doll and disintegrated.

They learned quickly that the things turned to dust when they died. Soon a layer three inches thick coated the ground, mixing with the snow. It covered Penelope's face and clothing. The Embraced slipped and fell in it as they battled.

A Dominion grabbed a female Demi and sunk its fangs into her shoulder. Penelope struck out with her blade, trying to find purchase for its wicked edge in the being's thin side. It knocked the blade from her hand and raised its head from the limp Demi and hissed at her. "You're next, little Penelope."

Penny took a step back, recognizing the voice that had come from the Dominion in the dress shop.

Aidan plunged through the battle and wasted no time spearing the thing in the side. The Dominion hissed again and fell, turning to dust. The Demi collapsed, and then raised herself from the ground with effort. Hurt, but not mortally so.

Aidan grabbed Penelope's arm and yanked her behind him. "Come with me. We've got to find Gabriel."

"How are we possibly supposed do what we we're supposed to do in this bloody melee?" she yelled to him above the din.

He shook his head. "I don't know, Penny. I don't know."

They spotted Gabriel and worked their way over to him. Aidan ruthlessly cut down any Dominion in their path along the way.

Gabriel flipped one of the creatures to the ground and stabbed it. He stood, his black hair and cloak swirling around him and his blue eyes lit with bloodlust. "The circle. Get to the circle." He pointed toward an old warehouse that stood near the doorway. The Demi and Vampir had made a half-circle around it and appeared to be defending the perimeter. There, the snow remained pristine. No Dominion ash tainted it.

Aidan pulled her toward it.

"Aidan," called Gabriel.

He stopped and turned.

"Remember to spill her blood."

Chapter Eleven

In the chaos and the tumult, they came together.

All around them the Demi and Embraced formed a half circle, fighting the Dominion, and creating the eye of the storm in which Aidan and Penelope now stood. The wall of the building formed the other part of the place of peace.

Once they'd stepped into the area, the sounds of battle had receded until they sounded a mile away. The air was warmer too.

Even so, Penelope wasn't much in the mood for the task at hand.

Aidan walked toward her slowly, his eyes dark and intense. He stood a breath's space away without touching her. Finally, he reached out and wiped a tear from her cheek with the flat of his thumb.

"I know what you're thinking, but we have to do this, you know," he murmured. "We have to forget what's going on around us and concentrate only on each other." He reached out and slipped her coat off, and then the edge of her dress over her shoulder. "Are you going to let me make love to you? I do love you, you know."

Her eyes narrowed. "You confuse me."

He snaked his arm around her waist and drew her against him. "Shhh...just don't think right now, Penny. Just feel."

Her breath caught and grew heavier. God, how she wanted him. She wished like hell he wanted her, too. Not out of a sense of responsibility, but simply because he loved her. Her heart squeezed painfully. And he *didn't* love her. He'd said that only to make it easier for her to come to him. No one loved her. That was far too much to ask. Her father hadn't loved her no matter how she'd tried to please him, and Aidan didn't love her either.

She closed her eyes for a moment, steadying herself. When she opened them, she made sure it was anger that flashed there and not the overwhelming sorrow she felt. "Don't call it that. Don't call it *making love*. You can fuck me, yes. You can fuck me because you have to. I don't have a choice here. I'm the sacrificial la—"

His eyes flashed dangerously. "Fine. I'll fuck you *and* make love to you." His hot mouth came down on hers, demanding she open to him. He slid his tongue into her mouth, and she closed her eyes as it swiped against hers.

The air around them tingled as the powerful spell binding them wove itself. Her sex began to respond to him. Her nipples tightened. He didn't bother with the buttons on her dress, but simply rent the fabric. She heard the buttons pop and fly, and her dress slithered down her aroused body and pooled at her feet, leaving her in her corset and stockings.

Aidan's eyes darkened as they roved her scantily clad body. She felt his muscles tighten. She reached out and unbuttoned his shirt. It drifted to the ground, revealing his chest, arms, and stomach in all their glory.

He frowned. "Are you cold?"

She shook her head. She hadn't even noticed the temperature. Then she realized it felt warmer in the circle than it should. Was it because of them? Because they were two halves of the One, starting the process that would make them whole?

She looked down. The snow had melted and the ground had dried. "Aidan?"

"It's whatever...." He trailed off and shook his head. "I don't know what it is, and it's not important right now. Only this matters." He unlaced her corset and let it fall away.

He twined his arm around the small of her back and drew her against him. Lowering his head, he sucked at her nipple. His tongue found every nook and cranny of the hardened nub and drew a shuddering sigh from her.

Aidan knelt and removed her boots, stockings, and undergarment. When she was bared to him, he parted her legs and licked at the apex of her thighs, laving her clit. Penelope's hands tightened on his shoulders.

"I wish I could take my time with you," he murmured against her mound.

She rubbed her wet and swollen sex against his mouth. "Just go ahead and fuck me," she whispered.

Penelope couldn't say how he lost all his clothing. Before she knew it, he'd moved her near the wall of the warehouse and pushed her against it. He rubbed the hard length of his body against hers, and then lifted her. She twined her legs around his waist. With one hard thrust, he impaled her and she cried out in ecstasy. She bit his shoulder hard enough to draw blood.

"God, yes, Aidan. That feels so good," she murmured against his skin.

He grunted in response and began to work his cock in and out of her. She imagined how she must look, her legs wrapped around him and his buttocks clenching with every thrust into her warm body. Penelope felt every ridge of his hard cock, every centimeter of its length as it slid in and out of her, massaging the walls of her pussy.

The tempo increased until he was thrusting into her with his whole length, harder and faster, pressing the small of her back against the wall with every entry. Dimly, she noted that it hurt to have her back pressed against the brick. That pain was dwarfed in comparison to the pleasure Aidan gave her. Still, she couldn't help wincing.

"Your back," he said.

"It's all right."

"No." He pulled her away from the wall and set her to her feet. He ran his fingers over the scratches. "I'm so sorry, Penny. I never want to hurt you. I hope you understand that." With loving care, he licked the length of each wound he'd made and the pain disappeared.

Penelope turned toward him and pulled him against her. Tears stung her eyes. She wanted to break down and tell him how much she loved him. But her pride would pay for that folly later.

"Aidan, make love to me," she choked out instead. "Please…make love to me. I don't even care if it's a lie." She buried her face in his neck so he couldn't see her expression.

He scooped her up in his arms and laid her down in the center of the circle. After he positioned himself between her thighs, he looked down at her as he thrust into her body. His eyes were a dark midnight blue, completely without pupils. Perspiration coated them both. She watched as it dripped down Aidan's chest.

He thrust slowly at first, and then faster and harder. She caught his rhythm and matched him stroke for stroke. Her climax built inexorably. She reached out on either side of her, wanting to grasp something, anything against the tide of sensation that rose in her and threatened to overwhelm.

Aidan put his hands to her waist and pulled her up into a sitting position. Now his body rubbed at her clit and his cock brushed at the sensitive spot deep within her.

His mind brushed against hers and asked for permission to enter. Penelope opened up to him fully. Their minds flirted, caressed each other, and then locked. She could feel what he felt—his cock sliding in and out of her tight, wet heat. How her muscles gripped his length. She felt how much he enjoyed the feel of her soft bare skin against his, her cries of pleasure. She gasped as the tidal wave began to flow over her.

He arched his neck in invitation and she bit. He groaned in satisfaction, and she felt the ecstasy her bite provided him. He was ready to come.

Aidan grasped her hair firmly and exposed her throat. His fangs sunk deep. The feel of his mouth on her neck, his teeth sinking into her was beyond euphoric.

Their minds, their sex, their veins were connected. Their shared blood coursed through their very hearts. They were truly one.

Penelope came.

Groaning, Aidan removed his mouth and thrust hard and deep within her, a hot stream of his seed bathing her womb. Blood coursed from the wound at her throat and trickled to the ground beneath them. Still, she climaxed. Her sex pulsed and throbbed around his cock and she tried to concentrate on holding her neck taut, allowing her blood to drop onto the ground.

Finally, the pleasurable waves of their shared orgasm slowed. Aidan pulled her to him and licked her wound, cleaning up the blood. "I'm sorry, Penny," he murmured. "I'm so sorry if I hurt you."

He shifted and cradled her in his lap. She tucked her head between his jaw and shoulder and relaxed. For a moment she forgot she was supposed to hate him. God…why couldn't she hate him?

"It's all right," she whispered. "It's all right. You didn't hurt me." Not physically, at least.

She felt a blanket drape her and she raised her head to see Niccolo's concerned face. "Are you hurt, *mia cara*?"

Penelope shook her head and looked around. The Dominion were gone, the doorway was closed. The Demi and the Embraced stood around them, some injured, some bloody. Not all of them present. They stared down at them.

"It worked," breathed Aidan.

Gabriel stepped forward. He was covered in ash. "It worked."

Charlie appeared beside Gabriel. He looked angry. Penelope felt sorry for him. She knew well he loved her, and he'd just had to watch her have sex with another man.

Penelope pulled herself from Aidan's lap and, wrapping herself in the blanket, put some distance between herself and Aidan. There was no reason to rub salt in Charlie's wound. And, in any case, it hurt to be held by Aidan. No reason to stay where she wasn't wanted.

She went to Charlie and he wrapped her in his arms. She didn't look back at Aidan, but she could feel his hot gaze on her back.

* * * * *

Gabriel leaned back in his chair and unfolded his newspaper. Twilight shone in through the window of the Sugar Jar's parlor. He sighed in contentment. Everything was calm and back to normal. At least, for a little while.

The Dominion would be far away now. The veil was thick after the equinox and Aidan and Penelope's act as the One had sealed the door much more securely than Gabriel had ever dreamed. They shared a deep love, a bond like only most could imagine. If only they would realize it.

He flipped the edge of his newspaper straight and raked his gaze across the front page of the paper. *Vampires alive and well in New York City* read the headline.

Not merely a horror story.

Yesterday evening a bizarre sight was beheld as two strange factions battled each other to the death. Ghost like creatures that could only be described as ghouls fought against what spectators describe as real, live vampires....

The story went on to summarize the skirmish, although the reporters had missed the strange sexual ritual that had taken place during its midst. The article did report that the vampires had apparently won the battle and went on to muse about what that meant for the city of New York.

The door opened a bit wider and Kara padded in on her delicate feet. She sat in front of him and looked up expectantly with her sly green eyes. Gabriel patted his lap. She jumped onto it, unmindful of the fact that she now laid directly on his newspaper, successfully impeding his ability to read it.

"Looks as if we've been outed, friend," Gabriel said to the cat.

"That we have," said Niccolo from the doorway. "I've been out since early afternoon. The streets are abuzz with the news."

Niccolo walked to stand in front of him, clasping his hands at the small of his back. His expression was stoic—unreadable as always. "Some say it is lies, others say not. Everyone who believes they have had an encounter with one of the Vampir is spouting off about it now. You should hear the tales, my friend. We are grotesque, rotting monsters that steal babies from their cribs and suck them dry of their blood. We appear in graveyards at night, freshly risen from our graves and smelling of decaying flesh and soil."

Gabriel retrieved his newspaper from under Kara's generous backside, closed it and set it on the table beside him. "Hmm...well. That's not good public relations, is it?"

"No. But better they believe these impossible stories than the truth."

"We'll keep a low profile for a while. This story will fade, you'll see. They'll forget about this nonsense, chalk it up to mass hallucination and the fevered imagination of a reporter. Human minds can be counted upon to rationalize anything away."

Gabriel reached down to pet Kara and stopped short, his gaze catching on a small article on the back page of the newspaper. He stroked Kara's silken fur just behind one ear as he read.

Reward Offered

Wilhelmina and Therese Pierce of Hartford, Connecticut desperately seek lost niece, Penelope Agnes Coddington. Missing since early December, Miss Coddington, a lady of quality, had been traveling from England to reside with her great-aunts when she disappeared. Miss Coddington is twenty-two years old with reddish-blond hair and blue-green eyes. Any information regarding her whereabouts should be provided to the New York City Police Department. Any information directly leading to her retrieval shall be richly rewarded.

* * * * *

Aidan stuffed the last of his shirts into his pack and closed it. It was time to get away from here, time to leave New York and do what he'd set out to do. Gabriel had rewarded him handsomely for the role he'd played in closing the door on the Dominion and helping him out around the Sugar Jar. Gabriel had given him far more than Aidan had ever had in his life. It was a stake of money large enough to get him west, buy land and breeding stock. He'd head to Kentucky and have his own horses, yet, Vampir or not.

Aidan planned on paying Gabriel back when he was settled. No way he'd let another pay his way. He thought of the money as a loan and nothing else. All the same, he was very thankful for it.

A knock sounded on the door. "Come in," he called.

"Aidan?"

He closed his eyes. Charlie. He was the last person he wanted to see right now.

"Are you going somewhere?" Charlie asked.

Aidan turned, slinging the pack over his back. "Yep."

"Where are you going?"

"West."

"Why are you leaving?"

Aidan narrowed his eyes. "Full of questions, aren't you? It's none of your business."

"Look, I came here to talk to you, not to offend you. The way I see it, we've got something in common."

Aidan pushed past him on the way to the door. "Way I see it, we don't have anything in common. We're different as night and day, high and low, hot and cold. I have a train to catch." He yanked the door open.

"Penelope."

Aidan paused. *Christ*, that woman would be the death of him. Even hearing her name sent emotion through him. He walked out the door and down the hall.

"We both love her, that's what we have in common."

Aidan paused in the hallway and turned to spear Charlie, who'd followed him, with a steely gaze. "Where'd you *ever* come up with that?"

Charlie rolled his eyes. "Come on, Aidan. Do you think you're some kind of great actor? Everyone at the Sugar Jar knows you're besotted with her. It's in the way you look at her, the way you touch her." His eyes darkened and his fists clenched. "It's in the way you fuck her, which you showed most everyone on the equinox."

"You think we wanted that?" he snapped. "It was necessary."

"Yes, necessary because you two are bonded, two halves of a whole, two parts of the One. You love her and she loves you. Don't look away from me, Aidan. Yeah, I know she loves you."

"I was hoping--"

"What were you hoping? To force her to love me? Push her into my arms? Wouldn't I like that. I dream about *that* every night. I dream about touching her like you've touched her. I dream about holding her close and naked in my arms, making love to her. She won't have me, Aidan. Believe me, I've tried. I'm not through trying, either. But she loves *you*, goddamn it." He snorted. "Don't ask me what she sees in you."

One of the Demi peeked her head out her door, took one look at Aidan's stormy face and slammed it shut.

His heart twisted at Charlie's words. The fact she wouldn't have Charlie made him happy and disconcerted at the same time. He had to stop himself from dropping his pack right there in the hallway and going to her, asking her if she'd come with him to Kentucky.

"I thought she'd take to you because you've got the same blood," said Aidan. "You're both of the same class."

Charlie's eyes widened. "That's what I suspected. You thought to push her to me because you think you're not good enough for her. That's it, isn't it?"

Charlie walked to him, fists still clenched. "Well love doesn't work that way, Aidan, and I'm not taking *your* cast-offs. You go talk to her, right now. If she's going to come to me, I need her free of you. She's got to make a choice, but to do that she's got to be *given the choice*. Don't get me wrong, Aidan, I'll take her if she rejects you. I'll offer her marriage if she does. But I don't think she will."

They stood staring at each other, neither saying a word. Maybe Charlie was right. Maybe he should go talk to her, offer her the choice. The choice to either spend the rest of her immortal life in hard work, in near poverty, with a man not good enough for her by half, or marry into one of the most respected, moneyed families of America.

Gabriel walked down the corridor toward them. "Problem here?"

Charlie backed up a pace and smiled tightly. "No problem. I'm just trying to do the impossible, get the blind to see."

"Penelope is sought," said Gabriel. "I'm on my way to see her now and show her this." He thrust the newspaper into Aidan's hands.

He read the short article and threw it aside. He could see the future unfolding before him. She would be claimed by her great aunts, and while her reputation would be in tatters, Aidan hardly doubted Mr. Charles Scythchilde, a man of wealth and property, would be long in offering for her hand. Penelope would have a semblance of her old life back. "Tell Penny I wish her luck."

Aidan turned on his heel and left.

* * * * *

Penelope pushed the white, sheer curtain aside and looked down onto the street below, watching the pedestrians and carriages go past. Melancholy had overtaken her as if the Dominion had been feeding on her.

She tensed as she spotted a familiar form, broad shoulders swathed in a tan traveling coat, pack slung over his back. He headed down the street, away from her without so much as a backward glance.

"He loves you enough to deny it," came Charlie's voice beside her, startling her. She been so immersed in her thoughts, she hadn't even heard him come in.

"He loves you enough to leave you behind to what he believes is a better life," continued Charlie. "If that's not an ultimate act of love, I don't know what is."

"He doesn't love me," Penelope said bitterly. "That's plain enough."

"Oh, but he does," said Gabriel.

Penelope whirled and saw him standing near her.

Gabriel handed her a newspaper. "You've got a choice, Penelope."

She took it, bewildered, and looked the page over, immediately finding the small article requesting information for her retrieval. "Oh," she breathed. Shock stole her words.

"You could return to something nearing your former life for a time," said Gabriel. "Being human is not difficult to fake. We all do it. You can eat solid food and drink human beverages a little, though it will not sustain you. You can go into the sunlight, although it is not always preferred. As long as you feed the *sacyr*, there is no reason you could not take up residence with your great-aunts."

"I'm ruined. There's no way society would ever accept me now. I've been on the street. I've lost my purity in their eyes." She shook her head. "There's no going back for me."

Gabriel waved a hand. "Silliness. Society loves a good story. Some would shun you, but most would be fascinated by you. You'd be wined and dined and exhorted to tell the stories of your adventures over and over to the delight of all. You'd be the toast of New York City, or Hartford, Connecticut as the case may be, for a least half a heartbeat, until they found some other story to gossip about. Then you'd be forgotten, but still a part of the club."

Charlie went down on one knee and clasped her hand in his. "And you'd have the Scythchilde name to back you up. I'm offering for your hand in marriage right now, Penelope. Marry me and we'll take this on together."

Penelope put her hand to her temple. All of this was too much. She didn't love Charlie that way. The only person she loved that way had just left her. The irony was that she couldn't be with anyone but Aidan, even though he didn't want to be with her.

"But you have another choice," said Charlie, sadness clouding his eyes. "Aidan loves you very much. He simply believes himself not good enough for you. His rejection of you was simply a ruse, designed to push you into my Scythchilde arms. He was protecting you, Penelope, not rejecting you. He was protecting you from himself."

Images flooded her mind—images of playing with Aidan when they were children, how he'd tended her scraped shins and cut knees with such loving care. Then later, when she'd been older, how she'd snubbed him under Horatia's influence. How she'd grown colder and haughtier toward him until she'd finally cut him off completely from her life.

She heard Horatia's words from so long ago, *"He's simply not good enough to keep your company, Penelope…. You'll give the lad ideas above his station."* She heard him in the stables the first time they'd kissed. *"I'm not…."* good enough for you, she finished in her mind.

"He's gone to the train station," said Gabriel. "You might still catch him."

Penelope knelt and took Charlie's face between her palms. She kissed him chastely and set her forehead to his. "Setting free the one you care deeply for is also an act of love. I wish you much joy, Charlie, and…I'm sorry," she whispered. Then she was up and gone, out the door and in the street. She hadn't even thought to take a cloak. She picked her skirts and ran as quickly as she dared over the snow and ice-covered sidewalks leading to the train station.

Chapter Twelve

Aidan watched the train doors close behind him, found his sleeper car and collapsed into the seat. Settling back, he watched the steam belch from the side of the train, showing white in the cold winter air. He closed his eyes and an image of Penelope filled his mind. He tried to hold it there.

"Ticket, please."

Aidan's eyes snapped open and he fished his ticket out of his pocket and handed it over. Then he settled back and closed his eyes once more, trying to catch Penelope's image once more.

"*Aidan.*"

The voice came soft in his mind, a gentle, barely noticeable brush.

"*Aidan, where are you?*"

Penelope's voice, stronger now. Would she insist on making this harder than it had to be?

"*I'm here,*" he sent back, knowing she'd be able to tell where he was much as if they'd been in a crowded room and he'd called her name.

"*Aidan, open your eyes and see me.*"

He opened his eyes and saw only the bed built into the wall in front of him. He turned and looked out the window and saw her there. She stood shivering in the cold air, without even a cloak, looking at him with those big blue-green eyes.

He stood and made his way off the train and to her. "What are you doing here, Penny? Go back where it's warm. Go back to where your future lies."

Her open hand connected with his cheek. It surprised more than hurt him and he staggered to the side, and put a hand to his face. "What the hell was that for?"

"My future lies with *you*. I love you, Aidan. You love me. That's what makes you good enough for me. That and nothing else." She put her hands on her hips. "Do you hear me? I want to be with *you*."

Aidan stood, stunned, his hand pressed to his sore cheek.

"Charlie offered to marry me, and my great-aunts are looking for me. I could have my old life back, more or less." She smiled. "Until people noticed I stayed perpetually young, that is. But I choose you, Aidan, *you*."

Still Aidan could say nothing.

"Wherever you're going, that's where I want to go. I can send a letter to my aunts, letting them know I'm all right, but I want to be with you."

Thoughts crashed through Aidan's mind as he fought to accept what she was saying. She was choosing *him* over everything else, over money, over status. It was what he'd always hoped for but never dreamed to think he'd have.

Penny glanced away, betraying her uncertainty. "But maybe you don't want me. Maybe Gabriel and Charlie were wrong. Have I made a mistake by coming here, Aidan?" She studied the toe of her boot. "Forgive me. Catch your train. I'm sorry I came." She turned to walk away.

Aidan reached out and grabbed her upper arm, whirling her around to face him. He enveloped her in his arms and kissed her hard, his tongue snaking in to brush against hers. They drew several gasps of indignation around them, but Aidan hardly cared. He only wanted her lush mouth touching his, and her soft body cradled against him.

He pressed his forehead to hers and cleared his throat of the emotion that clogged it before he spoke. "I already know how you feel about horses, but how do you feel about breeding and breaking them?"

"I feel very good about it."

He smiled. "Wonder if we could track down Daisy and bring her to America?"

She smiled back at him and the shadows fled her eyes.

"How do you feel about Kentucky?" he asked.

"I feel good about anywhere you are."

Behind them the train's whistle blew, signaling departure. "How do you feel about getting on this train with me right now?"

"Hmmm...." She pursed her lips and feigned deep thought. "Do you have a private sleeper car?"

He laughed. "Yes."

Her smile widened. "Then I feel very, very good about that."

"You're mine, Penny, and I'm never letting you go again. Not for eternity."

About the author:

Anya Bast writes erotic fantasy & paranormal romance. Primarily, she writes happily-ever-afters with lots of steamy sex. After all, how can you have a happily-ever-after without lots of sex?

Anya welcomes mail from readers. You can write to her c/o Ellora's Cave Publishing at 1337 Commerce Drive, Suite 13, Stow OH 44224.

Also by Anya Bast:

Why an electronic book?

We live in the Information Age — an exciting time in the history of human civilization in which technology rules supreme and continues to progress in leaps and bounds every minute of every hour of every day. For a multitude of reasons, more and more avid literary fans are opting to purchase e-books instead of paperbacks. The question to those not yet initiated to the world of electronic reading is simply: *why?*

1. *Price.* An electronic title at Ellora's Cave Publishing runs anywhere from 40-75% less than the cover price of the <u>exact same title</u> in paperback format. Why? Cold mathematics. It is less expensive to publish an e-book than it is to publish a paperback, so the savings are passed along to the consumer.

2. *Space.* Running out of room to house your paperback books? That is one worry you will never have with electronic novels. For a low one-time cost, you can purchase a handheld computer designed specifically for e-reading purposes. Many e-readers are larger than the average handheld, giving you plenty of screen room. Better yet, hundreds of titles can be stored within your new library — a single

microchip. (Please note that Ellora's Cave does not endorse any specific brands. You can check our website at www.ellorascave.com for customer recommendations we make available to new consumers.)

3. *Mobility.* Because your new library now consists of only a microchip, your entire cache of books can be taken with you wherever you go.

4. *Personal preferences are accounted for.* Are the words you are currently reading too small? Too large? Too...**ANNOYING**? Paperback books cannot be modified according to personal preferences, but e-books can.

5. *Innovation.* The way you read a book is not the only advancement the Information Age has gifted the literary community with. There is also the factor of what you can read. Ellora's Cave Publishing will be introducing a new line of interactive titles that are available in e-book format only.

6. *Instant gratification.* Is it the middle of the night and all the bookstores are closed? Are you tired of waiting days—sometimes weeks—for online and offline bookstores to ship the novels you bought? Ellora's Cave Publishing sells instantaneous downloads 24 hours a day, 7 days a week, 365 days a year. Our e-book delivery system is 100% automated, meaning your order is filled as soon as you pay for it.

Those are a few of the top reasons why electronic novels are displacing paperbacks for many an avid reader. As always, Ellora's Cave Publishing welcomes your questions and comments. We invite you to email us at service@ellorascave.com or write to us directly at: P.O. Box 787, Hudson, Ohio 44236-0787.

.

Printed in the United States
24661LVS00002B/64-765